AF191956

JOHN ANAKWENZE **THE SMILING DEATH GANG**

VOLUME 1

novum pro

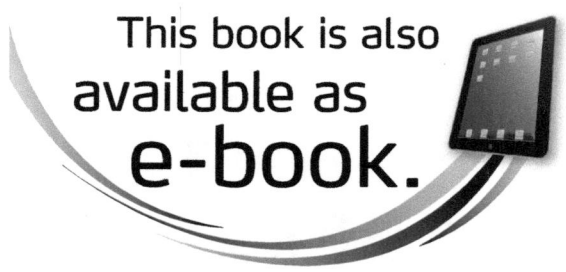

This book is also available as e-book.

www.novum-publishing.co.uk

© 2020 novum publishing

ISBN 978-3-99064-893-3
Editing: Hugo Chandler, BA
Cover photos: Potysiev Denis, Aleksandar Mijatovic | Dreamstime.com
Cover design, layout & typesetting: novum publishing

www.novum-publishing.co.uk

Chapter 1

He was ugly in every way. You could not look at him twice; all the same he used his unpleasant looks to great advantage. His face was broad and flat, adorned with small sized lumps under the skin closely packed together so that overall, he looked ghastly. His nose was so badly positioned that his large, flaring nostrils falsely gave the impression, when seen from a distance, of been turned upwards. His rabbit-like pointed ears were set so far behind and apart, that from a side view in a poorly lit environment; you would think that you were looking at a 'Frankenstein' rabbit. His face was totally asymmetrical; disfigured by prominent eyes protruding from deep sockets, giving the impression of staring. He was scary to look at. His appearance was intimidating and it gave him a fierce look. When the children saw him coming down the street, they tried to avert their gaze or they would rapidly cross the road, quickening their steps until they were eventually running as he approached.

He was tall but he walked awkwardly and strangely as he could not carry his long legs, shuffling along lackadaisically in his oversized, locally-made shoes that quickly wore thin, raising dust as he ambled along.

He mumbled as he spoke, making it difficult to hear what he said. You had to listen and concentrate hard as you made every effort to understand him. It would simply be detrimental to you if you didn't, for he expected you to follow what he was saying meticulously. He didn't suffer fools gladly. If you made the mistake of asking him to repeat what he had just said, he would strike an unforgettable blow at you for he was strong.

He was blessed with the arms of a killer. His palms were broad and spade-like. His lips were large and thick, with his upper lip inexplicably turned upwards, abutting his nostrils. The movements of his lips, as he spoke, appeared exaggerated and uncoordinated; this was not a good sight to observe.

People came to learn the unusual circumstances of his birth. His mild-mannered mother, while heavily pregnant, trekked for ten miles to reach a huge, bustling open market in another distant village to stock up on essential food items before she gave birth. She had lumbered along for miles and at last, now in the market, she approached a familiar dry fish section. She bent down to pick a nice, good-sized fish when the baby unexpectedly popped out screaming. Bystanders who had heard the popping and the crying looked in the direction of the sounds and they ran away. What they saw was too much to take. The newly born baby looked more like a monster rabbit than a human. His birth followed such a precipitous labour; she had never expected it that quickly.

When not talking, his lips quivered non-stop as if he was about to have a fit. Often, he tried to avoid the embarrassment by making a voluntary effort to hold the upper one still. He was named Nwadibia by his parents, but he never liked the appellation, so he planned to change it when he grew up, but it never happened, and his name remained the same.

He was bad in every sense – a street fighter and a wife snatcher. You wouldn't give him a lift in a car. His father taught him he must fight to the death and not to take any prisoners. As a result, he lurched from one killing to the other and he became a hunted man; a dead man walking. He was wholly a man of evil, a godless devil.

He lived with his father who was a prognosticator. Both tormented and tortured the inhabitants of a small village with a population of three thousand people. The two had dealt badly with the natives who they resided with, in every way imaginable. They were deeply flawed and unredeemable characters, unpardonably shameless.

Chapter 2

Nwadibia was brought up on the dusty floor of a tiny hut, infested with rats, cockroaches and all forms of reptiles, milling constantly around. He was doomed right from the onset for his father was the most notorious local prognosticator ever known in his native land. His father, Urdu, was surrounded by a countless number of wives. He was small with a protruding abdomen. He moved along at a slow pace with a shuffle, and appeared bent over as he walked, stopping often to rest and to lean heavily on his walking stick. He could be heard talking constantly to himself in a low-pitched voice. He was so feared that no one got near him as he went by. His eyes were so piercing that they could make a weak heart quiver uncontrollably to a stop. Children would hide behind trees, if they were lucky enough to spot him early, for he made little sound as he approached, and one could easily be caught unawares.

He wore short unwashed shorts and his white shirt had turned dark brown. He was seen constantly chewing a stick which he used as a toothbrush. Frothy saliva poured constantly from his mouth. He walked awkwardly along with no real purpose, other than to constantly think of who he could exterminate next. He was always in deep thought; obsessed with the mode of death of his next victim, often using unconventional methods. He was a complicated character who used soothsaying as a cover, attracting crowds wherever he visited.

•••

On one occasion, Udenka aged seven and his elder brother, Cletus, who lived in the same village as Urdu, were walking along a footpath early one morning. As they passed close to Urdu's compound, he suddenly appeared like a stealth bomber facing the two boys. Udenka made a quick dash into the bush and disappeared. His brother, Cletus, was bold and unruffled at the same time, with no inkling of what danger meant and he stood still, facing this most dangerous man. His heart did not miss a beat. Udenka watched apprehensively from where he hid in the low shrubs and he heard them exchange words. When Cletus joined him, he said that Urdu had recognised him from his looks as the son of their father, Francis. Udenka inquired as to why Cletus didn't run away, knowing how deadly the man was. Cletus said nothing, he just couldn't be bothered. Udenka found the chance encounter terrifying but he was happy to have seen this dreadful person for the first time. He could not stop narrating the story repeatedly to those who cared to listen.

Urdu lived in a compound of considerable extent, the size of two football fields in the middle of the village. The entire compound was well demarcated and marked out from the rest of the village by bamboo stick fencing, which was replaced every two years. The large space was rectangular in shape and well-kept.

Several huts were erected along all the corners of the compound, next to the fencing, to house his countless wives. The way he procured his wives would be obvious later. He found it impossible to know all his children and was unable to keep tabs on his numerous wives, and as a result, they conducted affairs and some of the children born were not his, biologically. They were from other men for he only slept with the newest and the youngest wife.

He would only accept cooked meals from his latest and most recently procured wife. Despite this well-known rule of his, the older ones tried to tempt him from time to time by bringing hot meals to him in the evenings, hoping to sleep with him if the food was accepted, only to be summarily dismissed and turned back. The other wives were completely discarded as if they never existed. It meant he only slept and interacted sexually with the latest wife.

The villagers witnessed frequent fist-to-fist combat, bickering and all sorts of commotion amongst these obviously neglected wives. He had very poor relationships with his offsprings, who also didn't get on with one another. It was not a cohesive community of wives but a man-made dysfunctional oversized family. The fact that Urdu was absent for long periods of time meant that he was unable to control things, and this allowed the tension in his household to reach feverish heights.

He travelled on foot and crisscrossed the whole region effortlessly, taking several days to reach his destination, obviously due to his mode of travelling. His only option was to get there on foot; vehicles were so scarce. He was to visit a faraway town called Okpu.

●●●

The news spread like wildfire and everyone prepared for the big occasion, excitement was in the air, at the same time they began to get worked up about the special visitor. There was a touch of nervousness among some of the town dwellers that they themselves could not comprehend. He was regarded as the best prophet in the whole region and no one had yet been able to compete with him. He was revered and yet hated at the same time. His name sent shivers down people's spines.

Preparation for his forthcoming visit went on for about a month, in eager anticipation of his arrival. On the day that he was due to arrive in the town, people woke early and they drifted down to the town square where the reception for Urdu was to take place. The crowd continued to build up and by midday, it had peaked. The square was now a sea of people.

There were women with their children, farmers, and various dance groups, dancing to the beating of drums and various contraptions. Titled men in their easily identifiable special costumes were allocated a seating position that befitted them.

Suddenly, the music and dancing quickened to indicate the arrival and the grand entrance of Urdu, his son, Nwadibia and the rest of his entourage. All eyes were on this famous man. The crowd looked at him in awe. The people who'd gathered wondered how this small man could command this degree of respect. With all eyes on him, he soaked up the moment while Nwadibia towered over him. He eventually sat down amidst the elders to watch the various dance groups displaying their various dancing skills to the applause of the large crowd of town dwellers gathered under the burning tropical sun, intensified by a clear, cloudless sky

The dancers came out in turn until a popular dancing troupe made their presence felt at the time allocated to them. Their effortless movements and heart-stopping singing thrilled everyone. The lead singer who was lined up in front was the sole attraction, loved and admired by the crowd. She was tall and blessed with exquisite beauty, dancing flawlessly with amazing grace. Her movement was fluid and very enchanting to watch. She moved in a well-choreographed rhythm but rather timidly towards Urdu, as a form of salutation and veneration. She got closer and closer and she bowed her head as a form of respect, but unknown to her or to anyone else this final move had sealed her fate.

Urdu gestured to his fearless son, Nwadibia, who suddenly stood up, and grabbed her with his huge hands. He pulled her down with such force that she ended up sitting next to Urdu. The people were stunned at what had just taken place, but they were unable to figure out the best course of action. They quickly succumbed to Urdu's charm. The dancers scattered and the crowd, not knowing what to make of what had just happened, moved in all directions in a confused state of mind. Urdu soon realised that his familiar method of picking a new wife in each town or village that he visited would be overshadowed by this latest move for the mesmerising dancer he had grabbed was the wife of a well-respected resident in the town where they visited.

Chapter 3

Urdu was feared for his powers as a seer that no one challenged him. He cut his visit short and he headed home with his forcibly acquired wife trailing behind him, sorrowful and sobbing. The town felt so humiliated and helpless. The elders speedily held a meeting in the dead of night and it was decided that Nwadibia who was the first point of contact with the lead cancer would be hunted down and eliminated. They debated and debated into the night on who in the town was the most suitable to carry out the onerous job of finishing off the ugly one. Eventually the town crier, Ezikia was nominated to hunt him down.

Ezikia had been picked up as a homeless child wandering the streets, abandoned by his mother. He was brought up by a local farmer who was uneducated, but he was hell-bent on sending the helpless child to school. At school, he was unintelligent, slow and was soon on the verge of being labelled an imbecile by the schoolteacher.

Once in class, the teacher had pointed at him and he asked a simple question of why Christ was nailed to the cross. He got up and started to cry and then he said, "I didn't kill him sir, I never killed him." He kept sobbing uncontrollably. The whole class burst out laughing. The teacher ended up trying to console him. Memories of his childhood spent wandering the streets never left him. He was seen often half clad, walking up and down the busy tarred road come sunshine or rain, singing, laughing and crying, all at the same time.

He had a loud voice, and that qualified him to be picked as the town crier. He was blessed with a booming, sonorous, blood-curdling voice. You could hear it miles away in the dead of night as he announced the village meetings or deaths. He often caused great havoc and consternation with his job as the town crier.

Not long ago, at a well-attended village meeting, he got up to speak his mind about a pressing topic that had caused a heated argument and he was shouted down by Fred, a local rich businessman, who called him a 'retard incapable of making an informed opinion'. This hurt Ezikia to the bone and it made him feel so humiliated in public that he didn't sleep a wink that night but kept on restlessly rolling around in his bed.

In the middle of the night, he jumped out of bed and the next thing he was out in the street to perform the job that he was well-known for. He was normally told what announcements to make by the village chief. This time, he took the law into his own hands. The villagers were woken up in a panic on hearing him crying and shouting on the top of his voice, as well as laughing, announcing the following, "Fred is dead, caught stealing, a bullet in his head."

In no time the villagers rushed down to Fred's huge, immaculately kept compound, barely having time to dress properly. The women, on approaching the house, ran faster than ever, and then they threw themselves at the gate, crying their eyes out and wailing uncontrollably; their bodies shaking in grief. When they eventually pulled themselves together and moved into the compound, they were taken aback when they realised that Fred was alive and well.

A second village meeting was convened in a short space of time to decide on what action to take against Urdu who had come from another village to snatch one of their wives, and if time allowed, to touch on the recalcitrant town crier who went beyond his job description. The villagers concluded unanimously that the two incidents were somehow linked up. It was the town crier who for seven nights continued to announce the impending visit of Urdu and they reasoned that he was partly responsible for Urdu's reckless act. Ezikia was to hunt down and eliminate Nwadibia, the son of Urdu, for he was the actual person who did the snatching.

Chapter 4

This unenviable task of confronting the ugly one really excited Ezikia. He went about telling everyone what was supposed to be a secret mission.

On the fateful morning, he woke early and he was full of himself and elated at what would befall Nwadibia. He brought out his locally made single shot oversized gun. He put on his worn-out, faded trousers that hung loosely on his disproportionately enormous backside. Ezikia was big, tending to walk along as if dancing, caused by his buttocks swinging widely up and down, out of step. He could easily pass for a madman in his trousers and bare top.

He trekked for hours, but as he approached the outskirts of the town, he entered a palm wine bar and there and then he began to binge drink for hours. When he was inebriated, he began to talk openly of his mission in the town. Anyone who could hear learnt the details of his plan; even the deaf somehow came to know.

Barely standing, he left the bar having exhausted all the money he had with him on alcohol, He staggered along towards Nwadibia's place, singing and swearing loudly like a drunk, with his speech now slurred and his words indiscernible. When he got within shooting range he hid in a low shrub, by this time he had stopped singing and he waited patiently.

He must have dozed off for he suddenly saw Nwadibia entering his house but when Ezikia aimed his gun, Nwadibia made a sudden manoeuvre as if walking backwards. His ugly face now faced the assassin with his facial contour now exaggerated by the full moon that shone upon it. Ezikia, coming face-to-face with this monstrosity, dropped his gun and ran off. His trousers dropped as he bolted, and the villagers who saw the tall naked figure running towards them dashed into the bush.

He kept on running, but after covering quite a distance in the direction of his town, his legs began to tire, and he went into the bush to hide. He soon found a safe hiding place.

Nwadibia, along with a few villagers loyal to him were in hot pursuit and they could see him from a distance diving into the bush. They searched and searched the bush in an effort to find him for thirty minutes or so, but he eluded them; his naked form merging nicely with the green pasture.

They formed a circle around the location most likely to be his hiding place and deliberately started a fire in the same way they did for animals who they intended to trap. The flames gradually built up to great intensity as it was Harmattan; the hot, dusty and dry season.

Smoke billowed up into the sky, carried farther and farther by the strong wind. Birds hovered over the smoke in excitement, screeching in unison. Reptiles including snakes, lizards and tortoises began to slowly crawl out to escape the blaze now swelling up around them. Amphibians, particularly toads, found the raging inferno billowing around them totally unpleasant and they made a quick dash to safety by leaping up into the air, achieving great height.

A few nesting birds left the area to find a new home. Insects such as grasshoppers, praying mantises, butterflies with conspicuously coloured wings and flies made a wise move to evade the bush fire.

Nwadibia and his partners waited in anticipation. Suddenly, as the burning dry trees now engulfed Ezikia, he burst out laughing loudly like a mad man, and then he broke into a song in his beautiful voice. Nwadibia was startled as he listened to the sound coming from the inferno mixed with the crackling sound from burning sticks and the chirping of circling birds. The long wait eventually paid off for their eyes caught the sight of a figure completely engulfed in flames as his singing became more personal. He sang these words:

"The ugly one must die! Die! Die!"

"The wife snatcher must die! Die! Die!"

"Fire! Fire! Fire!"

He came out of the bush burning, covered in flames. He staggered a few paces and then he fell, laughing loudly as his face hit the ground, hard. He died instantly with a smile on his unrecognisably burnt face.

Chapter 5

Nwadibia's village, called Akpa, was in the middle of nowhere, occupying an area of just four-square miles. One could walk from one end to the other in no time at all. The landscape was unevenly sun-baked and hilly. The inhabitants were mostly uneducated and not really bothered about adhering to any form of religion. One could assume that they worshipped idols.

The men worked as farmers, but the harvest yield was very poor because of the infertile clay soil and the extremes of weather. As such, men tended to farm in a distant land and could be away for months on end.

The women stayed at home to look after the kids, the livestock and to attend to the makeshift gardens. These women were completely dominated by the menfolk and they had absolutely no rights. They were banned from attending the village meetings and they were not allowed to speak even if they were brave enough to show up.

Their staple food was made from Cassava, a root vegetable, that was converted into various food items. The people introduced their own local laws and they held monthly sessions in what looked more like a kangaroo court where immediate punishment was dished out; not based on reason or proper judgment.

Men indulged in wrestling as a physical sport. Major disagreements were settled by a wrestling contest rather than by throwing punches. There was one massive quarrel between Nwadibia and a very successful local farmer that reached boiling point when both threatened to sleep with each other's wives, an act that was frowned upon in the village, and fraught with danger. It was at that point that the village elders decided unequivocally that a wrestling contest was urgently needed to finally resolve the matter. The date and time were fixed and passed on to the newly appointed town crier.

On that day, crowds began to gather in the arena which stood for a marketplace. You could see women with their children, carrying chairs and stools on their heads, walking leisurely towards the meeting point, tortured and made to sweat profusely by the intense heat. As the arranged time of mid-afternoon approached, the feelings of the people about the event suddenly became very intense. The whole place fell eerily silent; you could hear a pin drop.

Suddenly, the ugly one emerged, covered in slippery locally made yellow cream, making him look fiercely aggressive. He danced around while the crowd anxiously awaited his combatant. Eyes moved all over the place to try to catch the grand entrance of his opponent. Eventually, it became obvious that Nwadibia's opponent had chickened out, having lost his nerve to face him.

There was a lot of murmuring coming from the crowd, and to appease them, two young wrestlers were brought out to entertain them with their display of well-rehearsed wrestling techniques. Both endlessly wowed and delighted the gathering with their exhibit of the submission techniques they had developed.

The women, on the other hand, had no sports to occupy themselves with, as they were totally invested in household tasks and they performed poorly at keeping their mouths shut, which grated on the menfolk. All their free time was spent on small-talk, tittle-tattle and whispering; out of earshot of the men.

Dancing formed an important aspect of the women's existence and from time to time, they learnt new dance moves from friendly neighbouring villages. Seemingly, it was a well organised and well set up village.

The population lived in small family groups, and their houses with thatched roofs were widely separated from one another. The walls were made of clay, polished to a shine. A typical house had a low roof, making it necessary for one to stoop to enter it to avoid one's head hitting the roof. The rooms were surprisingly cool in the tropical heat; for the clay walls were designed to reflect the heat away from the house.

Obviously, furnishing was minimal: a mat on the floor, a few stools and a calabash placed on a table were all that would meet the eye. The population was indifferent. After all, most of the day was spent outdoors, as they were active and resourceful people. Homes were only meant for retiring into at night. Most of their time was spent admiring nature in the open.

Various festivals usually took place during the year, but the most valued was the yam festival, which was enjoyed in the early part of the yam harvest, between August and October. This formed a great part of the village tradition and customs. It was a time of great merriment, feasting and sacrificing to their idols. It was a village steeped in tradition still practised up until the present time; their daily existence was dominated and controlled by rich culture, laced with history.

The villagers tended to welcome the first moon. It was a night of joy when the inhabitants gathered at night in the market square to celebrate it with singing, dancing, indulging in storytelling (folklore) and making merry. But the whole affair was a sly red herring for a lot went on undetected in the partial darkness. For those in relationships, caressing and heavy petting often took place. It was always greatly anticipated, because of the sinister motives of the villagers.

••••

Once, a very naughty farmer was caught bonking another man's wife while the husband was avidly listening to folklore, close by in the arena. The virile male was summarily beaten up and banned from the village. The woman had her own share of punishment. She was rejected by her husband and sent back to her parents, to live out the rest of her life with them. There was no doubt that the most abominable and indescribable things went on during first moon gatherings.

Life in the village would have been quiet and peaceful but for Urdu and his son, both had turned this normally desirable location upside down and it was urgently in need of repair. The villagers considered at length what to do, how to implement it and how successful it would be. As they continued to contemplate and deliberate on their next move, something dramatic overtook them, putting paid to the plan of banishing these two unwanted and awful characters to a far-away land.

Ekpe, was a well-known and a highly respected, well-mannered wine tapper with many years of experience in his trade. One evening, he set out for his round of palm tree climbing. When he reached the forest, he clambered leisurely onto several palm trees with great agility and methodically set up his calabashes, hoping that they would fill up and be ready for collection by the following morning. He was also a hunter. In-between trees, he set up a leg hold metal trap.

Meanwhile, Urdu was in his hut chatting with some of the numerous children that he could barely remember, telling them stories passed on from generation to generation. It was just a normal night for him. As he began to tire, his latest wife walked in, carrying his supper on top of her head. The children scattered and disappeared to allow Urdu to settle down to tuck into his food without interruption. His obedient wife waited until he had finished eating and then she carried the empty plates back to her hut.

Having eaten heavily, he quickly felt sleepy and he retired to his bed. He was in deep slumber soon thereafter and the wives in the nearby huts were by now used to his loud snoring. With him asleep, the rest of the family felt completely free to wag their tongues; the atmosphere was more relaxed and purposeful.

They competed with one another and scored points on who twerked the best, the one who scored the lowest was very flatulent as she made her clumsy moves, forcing others to shift away from her. She made the atmosphere putrid, to say the least.

In the middle of the night, the women and the children heard a blood-curdling, scream coming from Urdu's hut. In a flash, they ran and surrounded him, looking understandably terrified by his bad dream. He gathered his entire household and he revealed to them that he had dreamt of his imminent death.

Everyone was downcast and they wished it to remain nothing but a dream that would never come to pass. Early in the morning, Urdu woke up his entire household, he wished everyone well and he then disappeared into the bush. In his twisted mind, he took the same direction as the wine tapper had the previous evening, in order to steal his calabashes that would now be full of palm wine.

Meanwhile, the leg-trap set up nicely by Ekpe the night before had caught a prey but not anything like a fox as the hunter had hoped for. The trapped animal dragged the trap along to free itself, ending up at the side of the footpath exhausted and waiting.

Urdu approached the palm trees in the dark and he suddenly stumbled into something in the footpath and he felt a slight pain in his ankle. He then walked a few yards and collapsed; his breathing was laboured and in a matter of minutes he had stopped breathing.

Ekpe woke up at his normal time, he dressed and immediately he was on his way. It was now daytime, so visibility was good. On approaching the first set of palm trees, he looked for his leg-trap only to notice that it had been moved. He followed the marks it had made on the ground, which brought him back to the footpath where he discovered an African cobra trapped by his device. A few yards away his eyes were met by the stiff body of Urdu, his legs stretched out.

Ekpe broke down in tears for there was nothing that he could do. It was too late. He was now distraught, overwhelmed with fear for his life.

When he learned the news, Nwadibia went ballistic and out of control. He rushed at Ekpe, and he hit him until he was dead. He then left the village and he let others to bury his father who had loved him and who had taught him his evil trade.

Chapter 6

Nwadibia found himself in a rather more developed town with piped water, electricity and a more organised system of existence with a rudimentary legal framework, which was in sharp contrast to his village life that had revolved around a kangaroo court. He slept rough for about a month before he found employment working in road construction.

He eventually secured accommodation downstairs in a two-storey apartment downtown, close to his place of work. The single room was let to him for a peppercorn rent. Unfortunately for the nearby neighbours, this building was full of misfits. How the landlord, who wisely lived far away, managed to pick these unwanted characters was beyond belief. In this detestable building, both the men and the women who slept in it stank.

Beatrice and Patrick were a young couple who occupied the front room. Patrick worked in a government department and he took his job seriously. In contrast, Beatrice was unemployable, and she remained at home doing nothing, she did not cook for her husband, yet she was a high- maintenance wife. All day, she sat outside on a reclining chair selecting expensive female clothing. After she had made her selection she would tell the salesman to come back in the evening when her husband was back from work to be paid.

This happened so frequently that it had become the order of the day; as certain as day and night. Each time Patrick got home exhausted from slaving at the office, he would hear a knock at the front entrance. On opening the door, he would be confronted by the salesman who naturally would ask for his money. There was little love in the relationship on the part of Beatrice, a dashing beauty. She would do nothing useful for her suffering husband.

Once, they packed up to spend Christmas in the village. Both loaded up their old banger and set off for the six-hour journey that would cover two hundred miles on a lonely stretch of road. The route was isolated, and one could drive for fifty miles without seeing a single building.

Patrick was a young man just starting out in life and he was on a low salary. Understandably, he drove an old car as he could not afford a newer one. They took off and they made their way slowly, down the narrow road that was treacherous and littered with hairpin bends.

They were driving for about one hour into the journey when the car suddenly broke down in a remote area, far away from the nearest town. What this paragon of beauty did next was out of this world. In a flash, Beatrice jumped out of the vehicle saying nothing. She flagged down another car coming from the opposite direction and unashamedly, without saying a word to her husband, she hitched a ride back into town.

Another occupant of this marked out building was Fabian, a tall, plain-looking man who had stumbled into money accidentally but had never revealed much about how that came about. He was not polished in any way as he had no basic education. He was so loud that you could hear him from afar. To add salt to the wound, he was cantankerous.

He walked sideways for no apparent medical reason and as such, he continuously bumped into things, falling repeatedly. He had thus broken some bones in the past. He claimed to have been born a prince because his father was a king of his village and taught him that as a prince, he must be different from ordinary people, so he decided to walk sideways. He was so full of himself as a prince and willingly accepted recurrent falls which he never considered demeaning. To make matters worse it was likely that he knew he was short-sighted but he adamantly refused to wear a pair of glasses for he considered it unbefitting for a titled person like himself.

Fabian was unmarried but he had a girlfriend. She was also an oddball, and rather than curb her boyfriend's oddities, she made them worse. Their bedtime habit was awful. The occupants of the same building and even the neighbouring ones suffered many interruptions to their sleep, as Fabian and his girlfriend were terribly noisy during intimacy. Both hit record-breaking noise levels. She would scream and Fabian would add to it by shouting at the top of his voice.

The record for the most disruption, though, would go to the new tenant, Nwadibia. It seemed as if he'd transplanted the sufferings of his villagers into this small building that he now called home. His room was on the ground floor, directly opposite another room occupied by a couple with six children.

The couple appeared to be normal parents, it seemed at first sight. Mathew was a gentleman, intelligent, softly spoken, educated and well mannered. The wife, Celina, was hot-headed, injudicious, irresponsible and wild but well shaped and elegant. She was also shameless, and feckless.

Again, and again, people were woken up not only in this strange building but in distant houses by a great commotion that often took place that was beyond belief. Hearing the screaming and the fighting that occurred during the night, the neighbours converged to hear what had happened. Celina, in the middle of the night, when her husband was fast asleep, would cross over to Nwadibia's room directly opposite for coitus.

On waking and not finding her by his side, her husband, Mathew would alert the whole world. A large crowd would gather to settle the problem, and the discussion would be lengthy. Celina would be warned never to repeat this shameful act, the gathering would disperse, and everyone would retire to sleep once again. This truce would not last longer than one week. Celina would cross over again to Nwadibia's room.

This same disruption would repeatedly draw in many people late at night. People looked at the human frailty of it all again and again. How this kept happening to a woman with six kids was unbelievable. In the end, Nwadibia was given an option to vacate his accommodation and relocate to a distant area or move upstairs in the same building. He opted for the latter.

Nwadibia performed badly at his road construction job. He had little experience. He was a habitual latecomer; the fact that his boss arrived at work much earlier than him meant nothing to him. He did not give a hoot about not being good at his job. His poor educational background did not serve him well in the position that he found himself in. He had poor communication skills and his accent was hampered by his heavy-sounding dialect. As a result, when he spoke English, you would think that he was a child who was learning to speak. People around him would look at him with sly derision, as no-one sensible enough would laugh at him openly and if they did the unfortunate person would be struck a near fatal blow.

In short, the job that he was involved in baffled him. It did not concern him in the least that he did not have the essential knowledge of the 7-Step process for asphalt pavement installation. To make matters worse, as the newcomer, he was given a tiny portion of the road to construct under observation, but when the observers looked away, he ignored the step by step process to get the job done faster.

When motorists began to drive on his roadwork, pot-holes began to appear at an alarming rate. When he was confronted by the manager of the construction company, he blamed the rain for ruining his hard work. He argued that the potholes were not man-made but part of a natural process. He also told his manager that he could not stop the rain from falling because even though he was powerful enough, his strength did not reach the sky. His boss said nothing but within hours, his job was terminated.

Chapter 7

Nwadibia was aware that his life was in danger and he was careful enough not to overexpose himself. One afternoon, he looked out of his upstairs window and he saw a lady, Agatha, carrying a basin full of oranges on the top of her head. She walked smartly, despite the load that she carried. She wore a long yellow gown and a red belt which made her waistline attractive enough to make her easily noticeable.

It was not what she carried that appealed to Nwadibia, it was her physical appearance that drew his attention. He rushed downstairs and out into the street to catch up with her. He told her that he wanted plenty oranges to be peeled for him and while she did that, he chatted her up. He kept on eating oranges, stopping the other people who wanted the same thing that he now enjoyed by intimidating them.

Soon, his stomach began to ache but that did not stop him from having more of the same and talking to Agatha at the same time. Eventually, it transpired that he'd almost single-handedly consumed all the oranges. Agatha did not realise that she had walked into a trap. Nwadibia asked her to follow him upstairs to collect her money. She had no choice but to follow him to his room where they ended up performing a sexual act.

Unfortunately, no money exchanged hands and she walked home exhausted and inconsolable. Surprisingly, she reacted positively to her experience and she became more drawn towards Nwadibia. She eventually moved in to become his companion.

The room that Nwadibia had vacated became occupied by the landlord's teenage son, Timothy. Nwadibia's previous room was directly below his new place upstairs. In no time, Timothy was bothered by crashing sounds that he heard at seven thirty in the evening, coming from upstairs, clearly coming from Nwadibia's room. The strange sound was preceded by screaming possibly as a result of excitement, it seemed to Timothy.

The teenage boy hatched a plan. He noticed a hole in the ceiling in his room, but it was too high. He began stealing cement blocks with his mate for days on end and they piled them up one on top of the other until they were half-way to the ceiling.

At about seven in the evening, the two boys took it in turns to climb up, helping each other to reach the hole in the ceiling to observe the source of the noise. They stood there and they could not believe what they had seen. They were transfixed by the sight of Nwadibia and Agatha in physical intimacy. Both discovered that Nwadibia crash landing onto the floor as he climaxed was the source of the unusual sound that had bothered Timothy for months.

Every night for several months, they climbed up to be entertained as they watched the unbelievably hot sexual scenes as they happened in front of them. Unfortunately, one night, their luck ran out, the blocks shifted as they took a peek through the hole and they came crashing down, making a deafening noise as they hit the floor. It was then that Nwadibia realised that he was being watched whilst he and Agatha were having a good time in the privacy of their home. He swore that he would seek out the culprits and torture them.

Sometime later, now out of a job, Nwadibia was at a loss as what to do to make a living to be able to pay his rent and his bills. He was made in such a way that that he was not moved about his current situation. He didn't lose any sleep over being unemployed. A chance meeting with someone who worked in the car park two months later changed everything. He ended up as a passenger tout in the park situated in the centre of the town.

He plunged into the job head-on and immersed himself in his work, using the most unethical approach to force passengers into submission. He ignored the carefully laid out job plans, and the red lines made clear to him right from the onset. True to form, he would typically target a young, innocent female traveller as she approached the park. He would rush at her, impolitely grab her luggage with one hand and he would then pull her along unceremoniously with his free hand, leaving her shaken, intimidated, terrified and traumatised beyond measure.

With time, the seasoned travellers learned the hard way which was to run away when they saw him around, and the wise ones avoided that park altogether. His unwanted attention and his aggressive behaviour had affected other facilities around the park as well.

A Roman Catholic Cathedral was next to the park. His presence had an immeasurable impact amongst the worshipers and the priests during worship. His timing was perfect, he knew the exact time when the priest was about to give communion. He would suddenly alert his fellow touts, mostly non-Christians (their beliefs bordering on paganism), and in no time, they would descend onto the church in the middle of the Eucharistic service in dirty clothing to receive communion, pushing and shoving aside whatever human obstacles were in their way, including parishioners standing in orderly queues.

In fact, a frail, elderly one-eyed lady who did not see them coming ended up in hospital with a broken leg. When the group was challenged on their behaviour, Nwadibia said that the broken leg was God's work. Even the priest was not spared.

He shocked the normally polite and educated parishioners one Sunday when the priest stretched out his hand to give him communion. Instead of opening his mouth or putting his hands out to receive it, he suddenly grabbed the Chalice from the unsuspecting parish priest, took all that was inside it out and put it into his dirty side pockets. He unceremoniously dropped the chalice onto the floor with a big bang and then he sauntered off. His outrageous behaviour knew no boundaries, for he had no conscience or feelings whatsoever.

His group of outlaws targeted the churchgoers' vehicles on the church premises. They were particularly drawn to the vehicles with religious emblems placed conspicuously on the dashboards, claiming to provide protection from the vehicle being stolen. Such cars disappeared quickly, as the group flouted such wild religious claims. For the same reason, cars belonging to the priests were stolen, often.

Innocent people genuinely going about their businesses, or worshipping peacefully in a holy place, remained at the receiving end of this wild bunch's actions. The idea was to make the small, squeaky clean population begin to waver in their idea of religion, Christian beliefs and the universality of a just God.

The attacks came from several fronts besides stealing cars belonging to priests. Up until that point, people could not believe that that sort of thing could happen on the doorstep of the church. The group even stepped up their campaign by stealing handbags that were left behind by the parishioners when they moved from their seats to receive communion. They were targeted by these ruffians who never missed such opportunities to become richer by milking the decent population of this small, sleepy town.

The landscape of the town was very uneven and arid, stretching for five miles from one end to the other. It was a decent town, arranged in such a way as to make it popular and attractive to visitors. It had a population of about ten thousand people, mostly young inhabitants, and the majority were government workers on meagre incomes. As such, they were at the mercy of burgeoning traders who gave them food items on credit, to make it possible for them to feed their families.

The town was divided into two sections by a deep gully. On one side, there existed a fairly flat piece of land, housing government departments, a specialist hospital, a large daily market and a residential area, while on the other side of the gully was a section of the town on a hill, occupied by traders and impoverished women, men and young children. This hilly part was densely populated. The town was loved by all because of its tranquillity and disciplined inhabitants, until Nwadibia reared his ugly head.

At that time, in the mid-forties, there were only three major roads, which ran parallel to each other. Vehicles were not numerous at that time. In fact, on one street alone that stretched for nearly four miles you could easily count the small number of vehicles and one of them belonged to a London trained lawyer called Eze. He happened to be the only lawyer in town, and he drove to court nearly every day on this straight road, and he lived in one of the houses alongside it. Even though the road had no corners, it was noted for steep gradient and sharp descent.

Eze was plump, of average height and light complexioned. His face was broad, featuring bushy eyebrows and slanting blue eyes. He wore thick glasses with dark frames that matched the colour of his crop of hair. He had a very polished public-school English accent, spoken in a pleasantly soft voice. He was so proud and full of himself that he treated all the people around him with disdain and did not feel the need to talk to his own people. He was undeniably hideous looking and distant compared with the other menfolk in the town.

Of course, he dropped the use of his native language the moment he got back from the U.K. and would treat anyone with scorn for addressing him in the dialect he had grown up with. He belonged to a different world yet lived amid his people. He did all he could to totally cocoon himself from his tribal origins. He went to great lengths to achieve this, dropping his native attire and the heavy native accent.

He was completely transformed and Europeanised in such a way that when he spoke, you could easily think that he was born in white man's land. He even told his only friend that he hated his name so much because it was in his dialect and that he would have preferred an English sounding name.

Even the way he walked was different and sort of imported. People around him walked about lazily in a crude, untidy way, stamping their feet heavily on the ground and moving in a most unattractive fashion. If at all they happened to wear shoes they wore out quickly on one side because of the uncharacteristic way their footwear landed on the ground as they walked. He walked as if he floated, with his entire sole noiselessly touching the ground. His shoes wore out evenly and his entire body moved together in a smooth and admirable fashion, which contrasted with the people around him, who threw their arms about in a wild fashion.

Eze had a large brown Chevrolet car that he drove himself. It was the best kept car in town and as such, the inhabitants initially craved to see it come and go as he rode to work and back. Crowds gathered as soon as they heard the car coming and looked-on in awe each time he drove by.

People would line up shaking their heads in wonderment. This was about to change very soon.

The vehicle took a very different form for this swollen-headed lawyer. It became a weapon of destruction. He was so feared that no one dared touch him. The police force was in its infancy and there were no real law enforcement agencies anywhere nearby. The town dwellers in that period in history did not know basic safety rules simply because they were not taught how to prevent them from being killed or seriously injured. They knew nothing about, 'Stop, Look left and right, then Cross'. No one told them they should never cross a road on a bend. Traffic safety courses or education that would have shaped pedestrian's, particularly children's behaviour was non-existent then. To cut the story short, the people did not know how to cross a road and were still incapable of gauging the speed of oncoming vehicles, to help them decide when to manoeuvre to the other side of the road.

Eze always drove at top speed from his white painted house to court in the mornings, tearing down the steep hill that stretched clearly for a mile, and then he drove back in the same way, late in the afternoon, running people over without stopping and creating mayhem.

This happened so often that no one questioned him. Maiming people in his path became a familiar routine that was constantly talked about by the populace. It pained them so much that they were incapable of dealing with it. This went on for quite a long time until Nwadibia arrived to create more havoc on these already tormented human beings.

Nwadibia was no fool. He already knew that his activities had turned the population against him, and that he would soon be declared a wanted man. One afternoon, he was walking along the road often used by the lawyer when he saw the vehicle bearing down at immense speed. Suddenly, he saw the vehicle plough through bystanders without stopping. He couldn't believe what he had just seen. Even though he had no soul or feelings, what he saw twisted his mind. His heart bled for them.

Chapter 8

The educated and well-mannered people of the town enjoyed the game of football. At times they were fanatical, filled with nostalgia and completely absorbed in it, body and soul.

There was a solidly built football stadium that had been constructed to a high standard. Its gigantic size was out of proportion to the small population it served. It stood majestically on one side of a long stretch of a major road in the quiet area of the township and it could be seen from afar, appearing isolated and lonely.

It was made secure and free from intrusion from outside by a twenty foot high, thick, cement brick wall that enclosed the stadium completely. It was impossible to see what was happening inside it. There was a thirty foot high solid metal panel gate, that allowed entrance to the stadium. It was strategically positioned in the middle of the wall, facing the street.

There was a Government recreation club situated directly opposite the gate, on the other side of the road. Here, government officials spent their evenings engaged in recreational activities which included lawn tennis, table tennis and snooker. It also functioned as a meeting point for civil servants, who often sat at the bar, drinking and gossiping. It was a men's only club, completely barred to women. This created much tension and discord, making it a contentious topic of conversation in this sparsely populated community.

Meanwhile, Nwadibia was fully absorbed in thought; relating to the event he'd witnessed on the road, seeing Eze, the lawyer, mowing people down in the street like animals, without even stopping. He was shocked to the bone. He had assumed all along that he alone had the right to behave badly. His hatred for the lawyer grew by the hour until it overwhelmed him. He thought it was now a matter of justice, dignity and respect.

He went to bed that night but slept very little, tossing and turning, muttering to himself and clenching his teeth from time to time in his effort to maintain self-control. He woke up the next morning feeling exhausted, and in a foul mood.

After a heavy breakfast of toast and ten eggs, he arrived in the park to meet his fellow touts and all hell broke loose. The first person he saw trying to find the correct vehicle to take him out of town was a young, slim man, so badly crippled by childhood polio that he could hardly walk. Nwadibia saw him struggling along at a snail's pace at that time of the morning, when most people were in a great hurry.

The man's whole appearance so aggravated Nwadibia that without further ado, he rushed at him, hoisted him up and threw him into the nearest vehicle, which happened to be going to a different destination a hundred miles away. The vehicle drove off instantly. The unfortunate man's intended destination was less than twenty miles from the motor park.

Nwadibia soon gathered his fellow, undisciplined, delinquent and unruly touts for the next plan of action. Gathering whatever weapon came to hand, including broken bottles, pebbles, rope, machetes and cans filled with water from open gutters, they marched down to the lawyer's house.

The enormous gate that formed the only entrance to the residence was padlocked and bolted from inside. They scaled the gate, landing inside the huge compound. Two security guards were quickly disarmed and beaten mercilessly until they were unconscious.

The group then broke in, found Eze still in his pyjamas and threw him out of the house. They then stripped him naked, tied a rope around his waist and dragged him unclothed into the street.

As he staggered along, dragged by the rope like a goat, the dirty water from the cans was poured over him. Crowds began to gather in large numbers, lining the streets to watch this bizarre spectacle. Understandably, considering his behaviour towards the townspeople, they seemed not to empathise with him. They couldn't believe what they were witnessing because, to them, the well-educated lawyer was a semi-god who could not be touched.

The people in the crowd were shouting and laughing in merriment, at having been so entertained for free. Not a single person felt that the rough treatment meted out was undeserved. As the touts continued to advance, a few unarmed policemen arrived but they were beaten back. Thirty minutes later, the uniformed men regrouped, brutally scattered the crowd and extricated the naked lawyer, now on the verge of fainting. The ringleaders were arrested and put in a police cell to face trial.

With the recalcitrant group now incarcerated, peace and normality descended over the town. These normally placid city dwellers had endured more than their fair share of suffering from this antisocial bunch; their behaviour gravely violating accepted standards. People went about their business unmolested, parishioners felt comfortable during church services, cars in the church grounds stayed put and travellers were no longer molested in the park.

All apparently seemed normal for now, but for how long? They asked themselves this question continually. Fear and apprehension lurked around the corner and uncertainty ruled the day. News of the impending trial of the culprits spread like wildfire and became the main talking point among themselves. The date for the trial was posted in all public places. It was also publicised by word of mouth. Adults waited anxiously and there was tension in the air; the anticipation was unbearable.

The high court where the trial was due to be held was in the area of the town reserved for the government, where most of the government departments were housed. It stood in an open space, facing the large city library. It was shaped like a town hall and could easily be seen from a long distance because of its shape and height.

It was a gigantic structure and dwarfed many other buildings around it. It was difficult to differentiate the front from the back. The side walls ended abruptly and did not reach the roof, leaving a gaping space through which rain and dust poured in, making it impossible for the building to be kept clean and tidy. The roof was made of corrugated brown coloured zinc.

Inside the building, there were long wooden benches lined up in tandem to provide seating arrangements for over four hundred guests, which was quite a number for this small populace. At the back of the hall was a gallery where people could stand and watch the court proceedings.

The large space outside the building stretched for a quarter of a mile and contained a well-kept lawn, interrupted by pathways. In between the open spaces were flowers in variously sized flowerpots made from clay, positioned in such as to make them easily visible. Surprisingly, there were no entrance gates or high walls to ward off intruders, because the location had previously been such a peaceful place, free from crime. That was, until Nwadibia suddenly arrived, to wake the city up from its deep slumber.

The court drew a lot of visitors who came to see and admire its peculiar old-fashioned architecture, posing for photographs in front of it. Hawkers abounded at the periphery of the court. You could hear them shouting on top of their voices to draw attention to their wares sitting precariously on top of their shaven heads; once in a while toppling over, scattering the food items onto the sandy ground, only to be picked up immediately and sold to unsuspecting buyers.

Chapter 9

The day of the long-anticipated hearing was like no other day. The major streets were remarkably empty, rendered bare. No human beings could be seen walking about. There were only two or three stray dogs. Shops were not open for trading. Creatures that would normally not venture out during the day became emboldened and announced their presence.

Rats could be seen crawling across the road; not in a rush as usual, but much slower as if they had all the time in the world. Lizards of various shapes lay comfortably and unperturbed across the lonely foot paths. It was no surprise that nearly the whole population had converged at the court.

Outside the court, a huge crowd had gathered; young and old alike, with children milling around. Inside the court where the case against Nwadibia and his gang was to take place, not a single empty seat could be found, the place was packed. You could not hear a sound, it was unnerving. The normally bustling city was eerily quiet, the town coming together in the hope to see these vagabonds dealt with mercilessly, if law enforcement meant anything in their heavenly township.

The gathering could not keep the flies away, vainly trying to swat them. Two cockroaches emboldened by the silence, crawled out from crevices and were stamped upon and extinguished. Suddenly, a child began to cry.

The crying went on and on and the crowd was already tense and irritable from the long wait. Slowly, anger became directed at the child's mother. Her name was Madalina and she was the most feared woman in town. Both men and women alike were terrified of her for she was a notorious street-fighter. She was tall, slim and well built.

Madalina was very beautiful and married to a humble husband, who adored her and regarded her as a very obedient and faithful wife. Nothing could be further from the truth. She was completely out of control, tempestuous, sleeping around and leaving her pants behind each time, as a souvenir for the men she had met passionately in bed.

Men who fell short in their performance, during periods of intimacy, were in for a shock. They were verbally abused and badly beaten up; leaving them with broken noses and multiple bite wounds in the neck that to the untrained eye looked like love bites which took a long time to heal.

For one young man, the story was particularly terrifying. He was tall, robust, and appeared so full of masculinity that he was picked up for punishing, spanking copulation. He appeared physically, sexually and emotionally attractive. What a letdown he was at the end. He stripped naked and as he was about to lie on top of her, he suddenly climaxed prematurely, unprovoked, wetting her pants that were pulled halfway down. In a flash, she sat up fuming, held the dangling appendage to her mouth and bit it extremely hard to good effect, rendering it completely useless indefinitely.

Madalina was as wayward even as a teenager, such that no one in the town knew how to control her. Her walk was so unladylike, that if you saw her from behind you would assume you were behind a man. It was not graceful to behold. She stamped her feet, throwing her arms about in the most aggressive fashion as if looking for a fight, which was a common occurrence for her. Her face wore an incredibly fierce look and she talked in a highly agitated fashion, as if in a constant tense argument, that would make your blood freeze.

The town dwellers would never forget one yam festival when, following tradition, women were not allowed out but confined inside the house when masquerades were out in the streets during the day. Men could be seen parading in the streets. It was unheard of for a female to be seen on such occasion walking along the roads.

She took off as if possessed and collected a few girls her age bold enough to follow her, cowering behind her, bent over so as not to look at the masquerades. Madalina paced along erect, out on the street with the other girls trailing behind her, and she was saying out loud: "let me see a masquerade bold enough to come near me and I will unmask you and break your bones, imbecile!" When the masquerades saw her tearing down the streets trailed by girls and raising dust, they quickly went into hiding.

No one who knew her well dared challenge her. This was to change in the tense courtroom. Her child continued to cry, and the people gathered there could take no more but were so intimidated by her strength and wildness that they kept on suffering in silence, but for one man.

He was a stranger coming from another town, and as such, had no knowledge of who Madalina was. He was ever so tall and handsome in a well-cut Italian suit with brightly coloured shirt and tie. He had a nice crop of hair. His shiny, pointed handmade shoes made him look like a male model. He was easily distinguishable by a small pointed red silk patch jutting out of the front top pocket of his jacket.

He moved quickly from the bottom end of the court where he sat to the centre where Madalina held her crying baby. Everyone watched apprehensively, their eyes fully focused in the direction of movement, their lips quivering. They held their breath, unable to handle the tension, which was at breaking point. Filled with trepidation, they literally froze with fear and panic.

Those gathered there concluded that he was pretty daring to make his dangerous move, squaring up to the wild, notoriously pugnacious woman and mother. He walked confidently to where she was standing, holding onto her baby and after both made eye contact, he impolitely said, "stupid woman clinging to a child out of control, get out of here at once." In a flash, Madalina threw her child on the floor with a seemingly gentle force and landed a powerful punch on the gentleman's temple, it struck like thunder.

The women in the audience gave out deafening, shrieking cries that made the people seated jump up instantaneously. The huge man shuddered and careened across the room before crashing to the cement floor. One could hear his hip bone crack loudly. Those near him reflexively rushed towards him, wailing and crying, "Oh my God, oh my God, she has killed him! What to do now, what to do?" They decided to take him to a native bone setter, twelve miles away, to set his bones according to the traditional belief that modern hospitals were not fit for purpose in treating fractures.

Madalina picked up her baby who was unhurt and maintained her position among the gathering. The waiting continued and the crying went on and on. A gecko was seen perched precariously on the high roof. It got so unsettled by events down below, particularly the persistent weeping, that it momentarily lost its grip and came tumbling down, landing on one man's straw cowboy hat.

He captured it and put it in his snuff box, preserving it for supper that evening. The falling of the gecko coincided with sudden silence from the crowd due to some movement noticed at the top end of the court. Suddenly everyone stood up as the high court judge in wig and robes emerged, flanked by bodyguards and other people in legal practice.

He wore a long black silk gown and a short wig. He sat down, and the rest of the entourage followed. Those on trial began to emerge, now led by the ringleader, Nwadibia, The Ugly One. They were all in handcuffs and wore white short-sleeved shirts and elegant wide leg trousers, extending below the ankles. Their legs were linked together by long chains which jingled as they shuffled along, prison guards by their sides.

The crowd breathed a sigh of relief, happy that at last this useless bunch would face justice for their dastardly acts. They truly believed that guilty verdict was inevitable.

The proceedings were about to commence when Nwadibia, a loose cannon, abruptly stood up and began shouting at the lawyer who he had roughed up.

He went on: "You call yourself a lawyer? You are the one who should stand trial, you Murderer! How many people have you run over? Pregnant women! Children! You, a foreigner fed on fresh milk to make you forget your native tongue! You call yourself a lawyer but have never won a case, loser! Wife snatcher!" What he was saying was met with deafening silence.

He went on and on despite attempts to shout him down. The judge could take no more, he had heard more than his share of rubbish and waffle; enough of the mumbo jumbo. He immediately delivered his judgement without any prevarication and sentenced the wild bunch to six months imprisonment.

They were taken away in a van to prison. The hearts of the crowd soared when the sentencing was pronounced, and they quietly began to disperse, feeling a bit deflated by the leniency of the punishment. It was generally assumed with some degree of certainty that they would soon be out of confinement to torment the inhabitants of the city once more. Their faith in law enforcement had taken a hard knock and they began to seriously contemplate seeking an alternative form of justice.

Chapter 10

The prison was situated in the centre of the city, opposite a big market and separated by a wide, busy single-lane road. It stood surprisingly on its own, in such loneliness, some distance from other structures.

It was located at an elevated vantage point and could easily be seen from any part of the city; such an imposing edifice!

A massive gate, the only entrance to the prison exaggerated its seemingly solitary nature. It was surrounded by an extremely tall, white wall, making it impossible for intruders to gain entry, or for one to view the constant activity inside the prison ground from outside.

Children from the nearby school dreaded walking along the footpath running close to the high wall, for they had been repeatedly warned by apprehensive parents that touching the wall would suck them into the prison compound. It was also hammered into these kids not to make the least sound in proximity to the building.

Inside this compound were housed nine deeply flawed and unredeemable characters { The Ugly one and his fellow touts}; an unapologetically shameless bunch. The forties was a period in the history of this town that was marked by lawlessness, a fledgling police force and an almost non-existent legal system.

Lack of accountability had corroded public respect for people in high office.

The nine prisoners had all moved to the township from the villages. They talked freely about the murders they had committed. Each made up a nickname to reflect various atrocities that had taken place during their violent existence. They listened to each other's tales told in graphic and spine-chilling detail, which surprisingly caused frequent eruptions of giggles amongst these quirky characters. There was no doubt that the stories kept them enthralled and entertained no end during the months when they were in confinement.

Lacking in feelings and emotional intelligence, they told their complex but tragic stories with ingenuity, flair and great panache:

1. Tony, alias 'Leave No Trace', was of average height, not at all handsome but endowed with well-built muscles, great strength and stamina. He was now telling the group about his murderous past. He had a gift for levity. This was the summary of his tale:

A well-known farmer, Okafor, popular in the village was going to his farm some miles away, early one morning. When he got to the market square, he saw 'Leave No Trace' loitering near the square. It was a chance meeting and it ended up with both agreeing to go together to cultivate Okafor's land, at an agreed settlement price.

They walked quietly, not talking much; Okafor was tall, gifted with long legs and tended to walk fast. His companion struggled to keep up, stumbling at times through no fault of his own. When they got to the farm work commenced without delay. They made use of primitive farming tools including a hoe and a machete to cultivate the land, as one would expect at such a period in the history of the town. It was hard work as the ground was hard and stony. Scorpions abounded. Sweat began to pour, drenching their scanty and dirty attire. The sun suddenly appeared, sooner than expected, bearing down on them, bringing with it an intense unbearable heat in this unfriendly, exposed, barren landscape, masquerading as farmland.

They now remembered, after toiling continuously for about three hours, that they had been labouring on empty stomachs. It was time for a well-deserved break to be capped with a traditional breakfast of roasted yam.

To roast the yam, a fire was made using dry wood. The yam was put on top of the well formed flames and constantly turned repeatedly, until it appeared nicely done and charred. This required a lot of experience and it was an art handed down from generation to generation. The charred part of the yam was scraped off and was then split down the middle with a sharp knife, ready to eat.

They sat in a small shelter formed by low growing trees to ward off the sweltering heat and ate their yam quietly dipping it into raw palm oil, laced with raw pepper and salt. Who knows what the experienced farmer said to his apprentice, but it struck some chord in him that made him snap. The results were deadly. Out of nowhere and in a flash 'Leave No Trace' struck him with a thick machete with sharp, shining edges, splitting the farmer's skull cleanly.

The farmer still had yam in his mouth as he lay dying. 'Leave No Trace' set the body on fire and left, leaving no trace of his dastardly act. Of course, he threw fresh leaves over the area after clearing the ashes; he did such a nice job and made sure he left nothing to chance.

As he recounted his story in prison, what caused much laughter was the fact that Okafor had roasted yam in his mouth. Even more poignant was the way the victim was burnt in the same way he had roasted the yam he was enjoying before he was terminated.

2. Efulefu, alias 'The Strangler' was a fierce looking and very driven person, argumentative, ill-tempered and a bit camp. He was such a complex character. No one knew for certain what he did for a living.

He had a small shop in a derelict building, if one could call it a shop. There was an old, dilapidated wooden table with three rather short legs, leaning heavily to one side. On top, a white rectangular shaped loaf of white bread lay on display. Next to it was a crate containing a dozen eggs. To fill up the table, there were three small empty plastic containers.

His private life became complicated when he found himself in a love triangle. He discovered that his girlfriend was also in love with another man called Ifegbo. Both men were known to be equally pugnacious; everyone expected a fight to the death. Surprisingly, the girl in question did not amount to much, physically.

Her manner of walking added nothing to her charms, for she walked like a duck; unsightly and obviously unpleasant to watch. People who saw her passing close to them often covered their mouths, so as to mask their amusement at her strange walk, which was especially apparent when viewed from behind.

Her face looked as if it had been run over by a heavy-goods vehicle. Yet these two men were in serious conflict to possess her. Efulefu, The Strangler, claimed he was a sucker for unattractive girls because he believed what they lacked in appearance, they more than compensated for in bed.

One day, Ifegbo was with a group of close friends, merrymaking and talking about things in general in a well-known palm wine parlour on the outskirts of town, next to an unkempt graveyard. The atmosphere was confusing, overcrowded and noisy with everyone talking at the top of their voices, especially under the influence of the locally brewed wine.

The mood was vibrant, and the cacophony was interrupted by sudden outbursts of heavy tropical rain. Ifegbo was about to share a story of his love life and the tense situation with Efulefu when the man himself unexpectedly walked in, drenched from the rain, as if he had just gone into a swimming pool fully clothed.

He moved clumsily but purposefully in the direction of where Ifegbo was comfortably seated. When it became obvious that an attack was imminent, Ifegbo jumped out of his seat and threw a punch but missed, lost his balance and staggered. He almost lost his footing, his arch-rival made a sudden move behind him and in the blink of an eye Ifegbo's neck was heard to snap.

He staggered and fell heavily, hitting his head on the hard floor, dead as a doornail. No one noticed exactly what happened of course, due to everyone being so drunk. All they saw was the victim trying to land a blow and falling. They all took his death to be an accident caused by the fall. No one realised that he had been strangled. The crowd quickly dispersed, the friends of the victim gathered around the lifeless body, crying, wailing, beating their chests in unison as a mark of respect.

3. Jabbar, was a smallish figure who loved to be called 'Carjacker extraordinaire '. He was a truly dangerous man who thrived on being hated by the rest of the population. He had a penchant for constantly repeating what he had just said. He was notorious, among other things, for crashing into glass doors, thinking they were open spaces thereby smashing his head.

Once when running from the police, he smashed his head on a glass door at top speed. It sounded like a bomb exploding. He had thought it was an open door. People screamed out loud in terror, expecting the criminal to fall; but it didn't happen with this wanted man; he just kept on running.

Astonished bystanders rubbed their eyes not believing what they had seen. He managed to escape from the police and had been in hiding for years. He only surfaced to join a group who had assaulted Eze, the lawyer under a false name. The lawmakers did not realise that the person in prison was the most wanted man in the city for a wicked and cruel crime.

•••

Philip was a young history graduate, loved by everyone. In his parish, he was a well-known altar boy and adored by the parish priest. He was ever so handsome and well made; such a dashing figure that men and women alike were fond of touching him as he passed by.

As a young graduate starting on a new job, his rich parents got him a newly furnished flat next-door to the medical students' hostel and a brand-new Peugeot saloon car. He was so delighted, over the moon, to say the least. He felt accomplished and as one would expect in that situation, he got himself a beautiful girl in her prime. Things moved pretty quickly, and both started to contemplate a church wedding. Events of alarming proportion overtook them and put paid to their planned marital bliss.

It was a normal evening. The medical students were out on the pavement facing the street at about seven o'clock in the evening. Cars were passing by constantly, pedestrians passed by slowly, and Philip was just leisurely driving into the entrance of his compound when out of nowhere, he was confronted by Jabbar who was pointing a gun at his head. The medical students nearby watched the dramatic events unfold as if they were viewing a school play.

Philip calmly climbed out of his car and was immediately shot at point-blank range. He fell to the floor, dead. Jabbar, in an instant jumped into the car and drove off at top speed. When Philip's fiancée rushed out of the house to behold the heart-breaking scene in front of her, her grief was indescribable and unbearable to behold. Most of the medical students were now crying their eyes out and could not be comforted. They displayed real sorrow, it was not confected,

The entire population of the city went into deep mourning. At the funeral, the constant crying interrupted the service and the priest who had watched Philip grow up to become the man he was until his untimely death, wept so much that an assistant took over to conclude the ceremony. A week later, the young priest committed suicide.

Jabbar told his group of undesirable companions in prison that, had he known about Philip, he would not have touched him. It was the only killing that he ever regretted. He had slaughtered several other people over a period of a few years.

4. Hassan preferred to be called 'Fire Extinguisher', only in name though, as it was the opposite of what he did. He was fond of setting things on fire for nefarious purposes. He was an expert at turning a small flame into an inferno.

He was huge and his height was out of proportion to his general appearance, his face was broad, and his large oversized eyes were too far apart, instilling fear into everyone who encountered him. He was ever so strong and muscular. His muscularity was an advantage that he used to perfection.

He talked fast, most of the time all bullshit, for he had little education. He claimed to be a librarian and bookstore owner, but no one knew for sure what he did for a living for he was scraping the bottom of the barrel. His so-called bookstore was a small, square wooden shack in an isolated spot in an unpopular area of the town. He never paid for any of the books he stocked.

There were four popular well equipped libraries in the city, but all had been torched in the past twelve months. He would walk into a library that was full of people, in broad daylight and go to the quiet Reference area and set a book ablaze, unnoticed. He would then walk out and wait patiently for the flames to engulf part of the building.

Pandemonium would break loose and being ever so strong, he would participate in the saving of the precious library books. Amid the confusion, the books he 'rescued' ended up in his own library. He took time to erase the library stamp on the pages of the textbook he stole. In its place, his own custom made stamp would appear.

It happened that in this town, unmentionable irregularities had been simmering for years in the very busy government departments; people knew that the top managers were very corrupt and more recently, things had come to a head. The top Auditor General, Festus, was appointed by the Federal Government to investigate the rumoured misdeeds that were rampantly talked about on the gossip circuit.

Festus was a self-effacing, intelligent and upright middle-aged man. He was married with eight children and still counting; for his wife was heavily pregnant and expecting twins. He had worked hard all his life to eventually climb to the top of the ladder. He was a sucker for early morning mass, had a great love for his closely-knit family and would kill for them if necessary. He always looked dapper and well turned out. People often talked about him in superlative terms as an upright man who never took bribes from the government workers he was investigating; there was no chance that he would ever do that.

The government building was empty when Festus arrived, as all the workers including the top managers had been suspended. There was only one access to the building and he alone had the code to a newly installed electronic lock. His office was on the eighth floor; an opulent, spacious lounge lavishly furnished and adorned with attractive paintings. His office table was massive, and he sat on an oversized chair next to a window facing a busy street below.

He worked for weeks on end, clandestinely at times and under cover of darkness, until the early hours of the morning, sifting through files and gathering information. Initially, his work appeared to be clouded in secrecy, his presence unnoticed. It took a period of two months before his identity was discovered but by then, working persistently and diligently, he had secretly taken away most of the important files under investigation.

When the top managers became aware of their dire, unsustainable situations, they were panicked as to what the end point would be. They contemplated hard for days, and in the end came to a final decision; a final, unquestionably clear solution.

Hassan the 'Fire Extinguisher', the most dreaded and callous individual in the town, was invited to torch the files containing so much incriminating evidence. He knew there was no access to the building, but fortunately for him, he was blessed with stamina and legs designed for scaling heights. He easily climbed to the top of the building in the dead of night and gained entrance through a faulty window.

Now, comfortably inside, he moved quickly from one office to another, looking for the filing room when suddenly he found himself in a massive office. On seeing that there was someone there, he immediately bent down and was motionless for a couple of minutes, breathing shallowly. The Auditor kept on at his desk concentrating busily on his difficult assignment which was almost overwhelming him now. Hassan, robust, huge, exceptionally smart and agile, crawled towards the table. Before Festus noticed that he had company, the intruder had by now tip-toed behind him and grabbed his slim figure like a toy. Hassan, in one fluid movement, threw Festus through the open window, and he fell instantly to his death.

The Fire Extinguisher moved quickly, eventually found where the file room was, he set it ablaze and escaped into the night. When he finished telling his story, he started crying while the rest of the emotionally impaired burst out laughing at how easily the victim was lifted without a struggle like a toy and thrown to his death.

5. Victor was almost losing his Christian name. Numerous people who unfortunately had anything to do with him preferred to call him 'Gazelle, The Bone Crusher' for he was ever so fast, lacking in patience and concentration and always on the move. He was now pacing up and down as he told his story.

He was a hunted man as his countless enemies were getting closer and closer. He had no job but instead of putting the blame on his lack of work skills he blamed it on newcomers from nearby villages, claiming they deprived him of job opportunities. Villagers leaving their homes for the small town kept going missing over a period of several months. The local Newspaper was awash with stories of missing persons as soon as they arrived in the town.

Victor easily identified them from their looks and the shabby way they dressed. Without any provocation he would chase newcomers down the street into the nearby bush. No one could outrun him. When he closed in on his target, he would fly into the air and like a Judo champion would hit the back of the head of his so-called enemy with his right leg, sending his victim crashing heavily into the bush shrubs. knocking him unconscious.

He was half normal, half maniac; a man of two halves. He did not stop at that. He would quickly dig a grave with his hands and a dry stick, and then drag his unconscious victim, dropping him into the shallow space he'd dug. He would then fill the hole up with dry leaves, sand and sticks, singing a familiar traditional folk song passed down over generations.

His last victim before he went on the run had just arrived, but unlike other victims, who did not have well established, wealthy families, he was lucky enough to have a well-placed, family members who happened to be rich. They were well connected and would easily be able to connect Victor to the crime because this time, witnesses saw him running after the newcomer. They were out to get him. At the end of his story, he sat down distraught, knowing now that his life was hanging in the balance, as the family of his last killing sought vengeance on a major scale.

6. Fabian, alias 'Doctor Death' now a serial rapist and murderer, had originally been a very decent, well-mannered, college educated technician. He was an old-time romantic; enamoured with sexy women. He never rushed but took his time when engaged in intimacy with them, leading up to the final act.

One day, for no discernible reason apart from downing several calabashes of palm wine, he ended up one evening for the first time in the bed of a "fille de joie". He followed his usual way of foreplay that normally led up to the end point but forgot he was in a totally different environment where time counted, indulging in activity regarded as time wasting by most streetwalkers.

The prostitute was so inflamed and irate that she suddenly trapped his balls between her massive thighs and squeezed so hard, they popped and with a loud ear deafening scream, he passed out.

When he got to this point of the story, he started to weep but the reaction from the other hardened criminals and murderers was unimaginable. They too started to wail, more so when he ended telling them that when he eventually married, his beautiful wife walked out on him unexpectedly after three years of marriage as he was sterile.

Soon after that Fabian began to murder whores. He hunted them down late at night as they paraded the streets in the dark, in search of customers.

7. The man with no name identified as 'Take no Prisoners' was the errand boy and bodyguard for the head of the gang, Nwadibia. He was deeply involved in all activities and took part in murder missions. Little was known about his background but apparently, he was picked up from the street, sleeping rough and with no fixed address.

He had a speech defect and was unable to complete a sentence without outside help. He appeared once in court and the prosecuting lawyer gave up cross examining him and lost the case.

8. Nwadibia, the master planner, had already filled up part of the story and more would be written about him. He was the overall head of this sinister group.

9. Tego was a young man of great intellect. He was ever so charming, amiable and measured in his ways. He was exquisitely polite. Tego had this magic effect on people who happened to meet him that made them warm up to him easily. He was a good conversationalist, never said anything meaningful enough to tie him down to an opinion, preferring to sit on the fence. He was not opinionated in any way. How this intelligent and well-educated gentleman ended up as a passenger tout in the motor park remained a mystery. That was where he met and got involved with this murderous gang.

He listened attentively to the gruesome, chilling narratives coming from these obscene characters, smiling with them and asking for any part of the vile narrative he could not follow to be retold. It got to a stage when the others began to wonder why he had no tale to recount.

Chapter 11

Still in prison, the notorious group's discussions shifted to a forthcoming event that was essentially war in the form of football. There was a match scheduled to take place in a few months between a local popular football club and a team from a neighbouring town. The two towns had been in a long running dispute for years, resulting in tragic loss of life.

The towns had become big enemies and each football match was taken seriously. It was always regarded as a fight to the death. Whadibia and his henchmen began to plan for weeks how to train youths as football hooligans, to cause maximum havoc and mayhem to the visiting team and their supporters. They agreed that it was going to be vicious all the way, with no holds barred for the unsuspecting visitors.

When the planning was completed, they swore allegiance to each other, and it was agreed that 'The Man with no Name' would be in charge of the rigorous physical training programme for the young recruits, to turn them into combat ready human machines.

Once out of prison, they moved rapidly, searching for people to train as football hooligans and ticket touts. They knew where to find these down and outs; a downtrodden and unfortunate breed, scraping the bottom of the barrel for their existence.

They easily found them in motor parks, new building sites, markets and job centres. With a total of a hundred recruits in their possession, a detailed selection process began, to find those with the will to become combat fit, with the raw potential to be transformed into ruthless and violent, wild beasts.

Height and build were essential, preferring heavily built six footers with frozen, expressionless faces. Spryness was regarded as important for a lot of running and chasing defined their responsibilities.

Several hurdles had to be scaled for one to become a fully-fledged hooligan. The end point was an initiation ceremony where many would fail and be dropped. It took place in the forest at the dead of night in a clearing large enough to function as a training ground. There, they were treated worse than animals with immense physical trials and indescribable tortures; the impact of which had far reaching consequences, in terms of emotional, physical and mental wellbeing.

Each person was lined up for an extraordinary test, using an instrument in the form of a seasoned cane. This was a long, hard stick, at least 5 feet in length and cut from a particular tree. It was traditionally used for flogging at certain festivals, like the annual New Yam festivities. It was also used to support other trees to help them to stand erect. The cane was processed in a complex way.

It was left on the low roof of a thatched house or over an open wood fire for months, to harden it until it was ready for use. The skin was then rendered rough at the edges with a sharp razor blade. A coating, using a locally made medicinal concoction in liquid form, was carefully applied to make it unbreakable and flexible enough to bend during flogging.

With the stick in hand, each candidate in the dead of night was made to stand up, stripped naked like a cow expecting to be slaughtered, and mercilessly flogged with two such canes for upwards of thirty minutes. The victim was expected to still be standing; his body all bloody and messed up as if he had been half eaten by a lioness, dripping blood from every part of his anatomy. His skin would be punctured at several points, a disgusting sight to behold, but for the pitch darkness that existed.

The recruit was expected, under such circumstances, to still be standing and not screaming. Were he to make any sound of distress or keel over, he was automatically disqualified, beaten up and discarded. It took the wicked torturers upwards of three months to get a hundred misfits well-trained in the act of violence; ready to pounce on innocent opposing football supporters.

It was the beginning of August. Now battle-ready, they lay low and waited patiently for the day of reckoning to arrive. The most talked about football meeting between the two towns had taken place two years previously and was unforgettable. The visitors were two goals up and seemed to be sailing to victory, but the local team managed to salvage a draw through a penalty kick and a 20-yard strike. The spectators ran riot when the unexpected equaliser came, and they invaded the pitch.

The two teams now about to meet seemed to be evenly matched, having an equal number of star players but their managers could not be more different from one another. The local team's manager was a colourful figure: a chain-smoking football fanatic who talked loudly in parables and did not believe in anything extraordinary.

The players under him adored and feared him at the same time, he had a choleric temperament, so quick to anger that a famous psychiatrist was assigned to him, as he sat by the touchline, puffing away at his locally prepared rolled up tobacco.

On the other hand, the manager of the opposing team was a melancholic, tiny figure; mild mannered and phlegmatic. Accompanying him in the touchline were assorted characters including a pastor, a jester and a soothsayer. There was always an herbalist by his side for he was a sick man suffering from multiple ailments including asthma, hypertension, arthritis, acid reflux and diabetes, to name but a few.

A few years ago, his team, who had the skill and resourcefulness to match any local team, had suddenly lost a match they were winning when three goals were scored by the opposing side in the dying minutes. He was so aggravated that he lost his signature cool nature and flew into a rage, triggering a moderately severe generalised prolonged seizure, which landed him in hospital.

The supporters of the opposing team began to arrive in the town in large numbers, draped in multi-coloured clothing and carrying flags and placards. It soon became a city of colours. It looked like an invasion. They were repeatedly chanting, "Loser, loser! Wife snatcher, ha, ha, ha!" in noisy chorus, punctuated with the beating of drums, clapping of hands and bursts of wild laughter.

It was fast approaching evening. The visiting crowd, restless to a degree, began to gather inside a large palm wine parlour situated on the outskirts of town. The building appeared to have been built in a hurry; the finishing was appalling with the windows and doors hanging loosely and in danger of falling off if one unintentionally sneezed near them. It stood at the end of five acres of land.

It filled up quickly with people, mostly the supporters of the visiting team. Loud, familiar music blared from huge speakers hanging precariously on the wall. The visitors gradually began to tank up. Discussions about the impending football duel the next day took centre stage and as they became more inebriated, arguments became more heated, the dancing became increasingly uncoordinated and a few careened and crashed, landing heavily on the dance floor.

The battle-ready local hooligans, knowing from experience the movements of their visitors, waited for them outside, patiently and unnoticed, choosing the most strategic and advantageous positions for a surprise attack. The unsuspecting male visitors began gradually coming out of the palm wine venue.

When a trickle became a crowd, the hooligans attacked the visitors in a most terrifying ambush. They approached the crowd like a pack of hyenas, flogging, kicking and punching. A running battle went on into the dead of night. It eventually came to an end. The visitors came out the worse for wear, sustaining life-changing and disfiguring injuries.

They initially stood their ground but because most of them were under the influence of alcohol, they stood no chance. They were overwhelmed by the violent and brutal force used against them, not to mention that they were also outnumbered. The local hooligans were well prepared and battle-ready.

Chapter 12

The long-expected day for the two football teams to confront each other had finally arrived. The population had slept poorly the night before, wondering what the outcome of the tournament would be and hoping that the home team would beat their bitter enemy.

They woke up early in the morning to the beating of the drums and loud singing coming from the football-crazy townsfolk and opposing supporters alike. In no time, everyone headed in the direction of the stadium, children included. It was such a momentous event, with adults fixated on the match, that nothing else seemed important; even food surprisingly became irrelevant, as most of the food chains were shut and not trading that day.

There was very tight security at the stadium as the crowd began to arrive. Such was the excitement that people started arriving several hours before the match was due to start. There was only one entrance to the stadium, and that was strictly controlled; only those with tickets were let in. The ticket touts were busily trading outside the gate and having a field day. They had never had it so good because of the high demand for tickets, which changed hands at four times the original cost.

Nwadibia and his combat ready criminal gang numbering about a hundred had other plans, though. As law-abiding citizens continued to fill up the stadium, the gang hovered outside the high stadium wall. They could not afford the entrance fee, as one would expect from a group with no source of income. The moment the football match commenced,

Nwadibia and his accomplices swung into action. There was no way they would miss the contest, come rain or shine.

With patience and care, they formed a human chain up the outside of the stadium wall, standing one on top of the other until they reached the top, in the form of a human ladder. One person would start to climb from the bottom of the chain to reach the topmost person and would then jump from the top of the wall into the stadium.

This contrived human device was created at various points on the wall; wherever the hooligans could gain access to the stadium. They were raining down like soldiers parachuting out of military aircraft into the battlefield, in a war zone.

As the wall was so high, spectators could hear the cracking of bones as the thugs landed heavily; many sustaining serious injuries as they landed. In some cases, bones could be seen sticking out. It was not a good sight to behold and an unwanted distraction from the battle taking place on the field right in front of them.

From the moment the match started there was such bitterness and hatred between the two teams as to be palpable. This was shown by the way the game was being played initially. Even a fool could see that it was played with great brutality. A clash in the first few minutes resulted in an opposing player being stretchered off.

The players of the visiting team became irritated and in bad mood, playing with such intensity that the spectators, watching what looked like a bloody battle, become noticeably uncomfortable and edgy, unsure how on earth this would end. They suspected the ending would be anticlimactic, a damp squib, to put it simply.

The sun now cast a shadow over the packed stadium. Birds circled the field, chirping and singing, looking down from on high, watching this warlike open confrontation. They sang their sonorous bird songs, as if to calm frayed nerves.

The supporters of the opposing teams were in separate enclosures and kept eyeballing one another, singing abusive songs intended to cause offence. Both teams seemed equally matched. Several chances were created, and shots saved by goalkeepers. Attacks were continual, with both teams digging in, twisting and turning but it remained goalless at half time.

At the beginning of the second half, a curler from fifteen yards created the first goal for the local team. The goal celebration was frenetic and extraordinary; there was even a momentary pitch invasion. A quick response to the goal came from the opposing team; a blinder was struck from ten yards, but it went over the bar.

The referee, a college dropout who lived locally, was not in control of the game. He was far from the ball in the final minute of the game, when the centre forward of the losing team flew into the air and nosedived in the ten-yard box, as if badly kicked by the local team defender. The mediocre referee, well known for his past failures, dashed down to the location of the incident and without hesitation, pointed at the penalty spot.

At that moment, Nwadibia and his team of hooligans invaded the pitch, stripped the referee naked and beat up the opposing players, bringing the match to an abrupt end. The outnumbered police force could do nothing; they just stood there and watched the outrageous behaviour of this band of shameless misfits.

The spectators eventually milled out of the stadium. This time, there was no singing, shouting, dancing or punching the air in triumphant celebration. There were no winners or losers. They walked home subdued, with flags held down and eyes wet with tears, reminiscing on goalmouth incidents, the dribbling and the constant booing at the referee.

Things gradually began to return to normalcy in the town. People returned to work and the visiting team and their supporters were homeward bound. Within days, the hooligans scattered without trace, knowing that they would be called back when similar situations arose.

Nwadibia returned to the motor park with his henchmen, only to discover that Tego had unexpectedly melted away. He had not been seen since they all were released from prison, a situation that sent shock-waves through them and they started getting goose bumps all over. They knew little about him or where he lived, for he had given little away during his stay with them in prison.

It was generally felt that the retiring police chief no longer performed as well at his post. He was incapable of carrying on much longer, due to health concerns. He was perceived to be too slow at bringing dangerous criminals destroying this historically decent city to justice.

He was so obese with a protruding abdomen that he was unable to carry himself. He sat on his opulent chair in the office for endless hours like a couch potato and rarely got up, for getting up was a struggle, but finding his feet eventually, he shuffled with great effort, panting heavily as if he was about to have a massive heart attack.

He sat close to an open window on the first floor of the police building and could clearly see the flow of people and vehicles along the road below. What interested him most was the sight of hawkers peddling assorted cooked food items. He would ask his bodyguard to rush down to buy food for him and this would be consumed without hesitation. He was never sated, so he had lost the feeling of knowing when he could not eat any more.

The moment he heard the jingling of a bell heralding the presence of another hawker, he looked down again to identify the type of food item sold; his ever-suffering bodyguards would toddle downstairs to bring up another meal; mostly junk food. Pedlars now knew from experience that going along this route and making a quick sale was a sure bet, knowing the gluttonous person he was.

Nine months prior to vacating his seat, his final action was masterful and brilliantly conceived, earning him much awaited respect from his work colleagues and the rest of the population. He was not a man in a hurry, excellent in intelligence gathering before nailing suspected individuals.

Tego was his office boy, tactical, adorned with a brilliant mind, deceitfully charming, and a complex, quirky character. He saw in Tego, a man of high intellect who could solve the perennial problem of getting on top of the criminal gang issues.

How Tego managed to get himself into prison with Nwadibia and the other gang members was baffling, to say the least. In prison, he was very focused and coupled with his good memory, he learned a lot about his comrades in the prison environment. On regaining his freedom, he mysteriously decamped from his mates.

The new police chief, Marcus, was a man of a few words. He strongly believed that to get to the hardened criminal gangs, one needed to be ahead of their game. He, unlike the retired police chief believed in rapid action, pre-emptive strikes and taking the unwanted criminal elements by surprise.

His current situation, unlike his counterpart, was now aided by Tego's detailed information gathering. He set himself up for a head-on collision course with these undesirables; decidedly on his own terms. The new arrival was a gentleman, soft spoken and initially thought not to have any weaknesses; but that assessment would be proven wrong eventually. He neither smoked nor drank.

Marcus was a Roman Catholic; never missed his morning mass, no matter what, loved to indulge in frequent religious fasting, a sucker for the game of lawn tennis played at a local court. He had so much respect for people and the downtrodden, indulging in charity work in his spare time. He was not a typical family man who had time for his children, for he was a workaholic, absorbed in his daily routine in the office, tackling whatever came to him, all in the day's grinding job.

Chapter 13

Jabbar, the carjacker got back from work one evening and relaxed with his family, playing hide and seek in the lounge with his two young kids. He took them to bed, as he often did, and read them children's stories until they both dozed off to sleep. He went back to the sitting room where his wife sat, listening to a play on his radio, while drinking a glass of palm wine.

They discussed the political events of the day. He eventually got into bed and the moment his head hit the pillow he was asleep and snoring. His wife joined him later as she had to wash the dishes and tidy up the kitchen, which had been left in a mess by the kids.

She was woken up in the middle of the night by dreamlike screaming coming from her husband. She was jolted to attention. Her partner did not realise he was making these strange noises for he was still fast asleep. It was a big surprise to her because she had never heard Jabbar shout in his sleep.

He woke up early, quickly showered, and then dressed in a beautifully tailored new suit he'd bought for an upcoming wedding. Donning a matching tie and a nice well-made pair of shoes that fitted his large feet, he was out of the house in a jiffy, saying nothing to his wife. He was looking dapper and well turned out.

He moved rapidly in quick steps, looking from side to side, talking to himself from time to time, as he often did. His left hand was permanently in his trouser side pocket as if searching for something he knew wasn't there while the other hand swung widely in the air in a circuitous movement as if suffering from some form of inherited disorder, like Chorea.

Suddenly, he turned into a side street, and after a short distance, he was inside the parish church which he had never known existed, as he had never been a church person. Jabbar hadn't been to church in a long time. He sat down alone, isolated from the rest of the worshippers. He was deep in thought; Seeing him, you would assume he was concentrating, deep in prayer, but far from that, he had never been a spiritual being and wasn't now.

The moment Mass was over, he approached the priest whom he had never seen before and begged him to spare him time to hear his confession. The priest doubled as a hospital chaplain and had received an urgent call to see a very poorly person dying in hospital. He asked Jabbar to wait, while he attended to the patient's urgent need.

The unforgivably ruthless criminal waited patiently for an hour, whereupon the priest returned and heard Jabbar's confession. Jabbar confessed his most recent carjacking and the horrible murder in cold blood of the newly engaged young graduate, crying at the same time, as he told the priest the story.

The priest, shocked beyond measure and speechless, still managed to absolve his sins and quietly left the grievous sinner. Priests are restricted from disclosing information provided during confession, so he could not go to the police to inform them but remained heavily burdened by the information he was carrying.

One would have expected Jabbar to go back home and change into simple attire, but he was not in a normal frame of mind. He ended up in the motor park in full regalia, ready to work as a passenger tout, along with his gang of fellow transgressors.

It had not been an hour when he saw an attractive, slim young girl approaching the park slowly; burdened by a huge suitcase she was dragging along. The moment she saw what looked like a perfect gentleman in a fitted handmade suit, she smiled broadly and immediately fell for that total stranger like a flirt or a tart, though she was neither of these.

It was love at first sight. He took over the luggage from her, dragged it along as fast as he could while the poor traveller wearing biliously yellow, comfortable platform shoes, could not keep up the pace. She called and begged the wonderfully dressed gentleman to slow down, to no avail.

Eventually, the distance separating the two parties was so much that Jabbar was now out of sight and gone for he'd been swallowed up by the surrounding crowd. He ended up in a nearby market and began to sell the contents in the suitcase, one by one. It took him a whole day to sell his wares, which included shoes, designer dresses, perfumes and trinkets.

He even sold her personal pictures. He got rid of the empty luggage at a giveaway price. It was almost six in the evening when he left the marketplace laden with bank notes and coins and in high spirits, feeling on top of the world; extremely pleased and happy. Singing a popular familiar song, he understood little about, he bounded into a popular nightclub situated at the other end of town.

His friends gradually began to arrive. He threw his newly acquired money about, buying drinks for all who cared to be spoilt in that way. The atmosphere was exciting ; the music was out of this world and the dancing became more and more animated, dancing their heads off. They were 'getting on it', enjoying themselves, having glorious meals dished out by the popular master chef until the early hours of the morning. At length, they staggered out of the nightclub talking and singing loudly as they were so merry.

Outside the night club in an unmarked police car were four police officers who had been waiting for several hours with Jabbar's description, provided by Tego. The moment Jabbar appeared at the exit, the officers jumped out of the car, quickly apprehended him and immediately put the gentlemanly-looking Jabbar in handcuffs.

Chapter 14

The following morning the news of the capture of the much-wanted criminal spread fast by word of mouth. Naturally, the city dwellers perked up when they heard the good news and celebrated it wildly. People came out of their houses, singing, even hugging people they'd never met before; it was crazy. In short, the town came to a sudden stop.

Offices were completely shut, including government departments. Girls surprisingly discarded all normal behaviour, embarrassing total strangers with wild kisses; they were completely off the rails. Girls who had for several years set firm boundaries on sexual conduct, now accepted request from complete strangers asking for a quickie in hidden side streets without any scruples. What a strange world the townsfolk found themselves in.

They were at pains to understand the rapidly evolving situation now confronting them. The men incessantly discussed the girls, feeling dejected, humiliated and wondering why, why, why women were so unpredictable?

Nothing moved in the city for several days until the citizens eventually decided to end the celebration. They realised that things were getting out of hand as far as the girls were concerned. Nine months after the arrest of Jabbar, the childbirth rate had doubled, compared with previous years, breaking the record.

The few maternity wards were filled and at times overflowing. Makeshift beds were erected in corridors to accommodate women going into labour. It was not the best of times to be an obstetrician for the workload was unbearable; stretching them to the limit.

One very popular and skilled obstetrician was given so much work far beyond his limits that he undertook to gain access to the theatre in the early hours of the morning, found an anaesthetic, which he used to take his own life. Workers and doctors came to work the next morning only to be told about his suicide. They were heartbroken; saddened that such a wonderfully skilled and popular doctor would suddenly end his life in such circumstances. Everyone who knew him, and they were many, kept weeping, crying uncontrollably and were heartbroken.

Jabbar remained in prison, deprived of family visits and kept in solitary confinement in the high-walled building. He was comfortably fed with fabulous meals, four times a day. The idea might have been to fatten him before he was taken out for slaughter. He gave no thought to the people he had murdered in cold blood being more occupied and obsessed with his small family.

He worried a lot about what would happen to his two young kids, now that he was no longer with them. He loved and adored his children immeasurably but did not give a hoot about his wife. When they were courting, he often locked her inside the rented flat, taking the keys with him, disappearing into the night and ending up at a nightclub. One night a fire broke out in the flat caused by an unfinished cigarette. His wife narrowly escaped being burnt to ashes by breaking a glass window to escape.

On the day of his trial, the town poured into the court premises. It was the second time in a year, quick on the heels of the trial of Nwadibia and his gang. It was now becoming too much to handle for these laid back easy going inhabitants. The court was full, not even leaving standing space. They huddled together in anticipation of the arrival of the most-wanted murderous criminal. They appeared subdued and melancholic as if they were still mourning the young graduate he had murdered.

The seated women appeared greatly saddened and tearful. Handkerchiefs appeared from time to time to dry damp eyes. The atmosphere remained very tense, worsened by the intermittent loud weeping. It was different outside the court, where over five hundred people were seen toing and froing, pelted by rain, talking in whispers and anxiously looking out for the arrival of the prison van. They did not have long to wait. Soon they beheld a slow-moving black van carrying the prisoner. The atmosphere changed immediately for the standing, rain-soaked crowd outside rushed at the van throwing stones and whatever else they could lay their hands on.

It was total mayhem until the police arrived to take control of the situation. Jabbar was nearly lynched by the angry, agitated crowd. It was a close call but the sudden, timely arrival of the armed police force, using tear gas to disperse the irate city dwellers managed to bring things under control. The moment people inside saw him enter the court, all eyes were on him, immediately followed by shaking of heads, as much in bewilderment as anything else.

Jabbar stood in court in front of the high-court judge, looking dishevelled, subdued and washed out. When asked to give his name, he answered so quietly that even those closest to him did not hear his response. Tego then got up to testify. When Jabbar first saw him, he rubbed his eyes to make sure that it was his cell mate he was seeing standing up to testify against him.

It then became clear as crystal that it was his pal after all who had turned full circle to nail him. Tego was a man of sharp intellect and attested to Jabbar's narration of events, leading to the carjacking and slaughter of the young graduate;

he did not miss a word. His testimony was masterful, showing his intellectual brilliance. When he sat down after his testimony, the whole room fell silent. It was too much for people to take, the weaker amongst them left the courtroom in haste, only to burst out crying outside.

The sentence was swift. The judge pronounced in a trembling voice that Jabbar was to be executed by hanging and the date was set. Jabbar collapsed on the floor and was carried out of the court. The crowd quietly dispersed, many weeping on their way home, the townsfolk were still hurting.

On the day of his execution, Jabbar was offered his own choice of lunch. He chose his favourite meal of pounded yam with vegetable soup, topped with freshly tapped, top-quality palm wine. He then lay down on his bed for rest and meditation for a few hours before he met his fate.

The site of the event was a popular seafront area called Star Beach which attracted visitors, holiday makers and locals alike. The weekend was chosen because it was teeming with people. The beach began to fill up several hours prior to the arrival of the executioner. Women in multi-coloured native attire danced wildly to the beating of drums, yelling and raising their hands in the air in unison, their traditional headbands drawing much attention from the gathered crowd. Their men folk sat and consumed large amounts of alcohol in merriment until they got so ratted.

Jabbar, in chairs, slowly shuffled meekly along with a jingling sound coming from his metal ankle cuffs. Behind him was the prison chaplain holding the holy bible. The moment they saw the most hated person walking at a snail's pace, the dancing and singing became more frenetic. This unexpectedly sudden change in tempo on this cloudless, sunny Sunday evening, unfortunately sent the wrong message to Jabber who stopped suddenly and turned to the chaplain smiling. He shouted to the man of God, "Look, can you see the celebration, saying; they have forgiven me, my people have forgiven me, I will smile to heaven, alleluia, alleluia!"

When the two got closer to the crowd, the mood changed as they started to scowl and abuse him. He kept on smiling until the noose tightened. At this point the crowd shouted to him, "You will definitely burn in hell!" Once the deed was done, they momentarily were elated, then they slowly began to disperse, their souls full of unspeakable hatred and aggravation.

Following the capture and death of Jabbar, Nwadibia, The Ugly One, and his pals decided to go into hiding, never to be seen again in popular venues. Instead, they began visiting less well-known places individually and never as a group, preferring to walk into bars and restaurants situated in suburbs further away from town in order to be less and less visible.

Their financial situation remained dire as they now had no source of income. They would send touts to their parish church to steal money from unsuspecting women's handbags. The thefts occurred when the women left their handbags on their seats to receive Holy Communion.

When the women got back to their seats, their handbags had disappeared, together with the contents. The women were then left empty handed and stranded, particularly if they had to pay for transportation. Some could not gain entrance to their houses because their keys had been in the handbags.

Chapter 15

Gazelle decided to go to his home village and visit his mum. They were so close that you could mistake them for husband and wife. His father, who was regarded as very eccentric, passed away when Gazelle was only ten years old. The only thing he could remember about his dad was his shouting late at night and his beating his mum up mercilessly until she passed out.

He was a drunkard and was out at the pub every night. Every time he returned smelling of alcohol, he would inadvertently urinate on Gazelle who often slept on a mat placed on the floor, as he stepped over him to get to the toilet.

Gazelle's mother, Ego was an affable woman who was loved and adored by her neighbours and all the villagers. She would not hurt a fly. Ego was tall and attractive and blessed with lovely long hair, sweeping down onto her shoulders. She walked elegantly, still looking young and beautiful, so much so that men still ran after her.

When his mother saw him approaching with quick steps, she ran towards him, looking excited, shouting and singing in praise of the Lord, for returning her much-loved son home safely. They stood there, hugging and touching each other for a long time, crying at the same time. If you were a stranger, you would mistakenly assume they were a couple deeply in love.

They sat down and chatted at length. She briefed him about events in the village, naming people who had died in his absence and talking about the wayward women who had left their impotent men for young boys. They would laugh and laugh together at her funny stories. She was fond of using anecdotes and parables to pepper her tales, often handed down to her by her parents, to good effect.

There was one woman in the village, a flawless beauty, whose husband was never at home because he was a long-distance lorry driver, crisscrossing the whole country. One day he left in his vehicle for a faraway place but, filled with suspicion about his wife, he changed his mind and waited in his truck in a nearby town.

His wife, assuming her loving husband was long gone, brought in a builder; a massive figure. In the middle of the night as they slept together, they heard her husband open the main door downstairs to gain entrance to the building. The huge man escaped through the window. Watchful neighbours saw him land heavily and bolt into the night. At a point, he began to despair of extricating himself from the narrow window because of his massive size

It became a topic of discussion and merriment in the quiet village. People could not stop laughing their heads off. The way the builder landed was so funny, half naked with his thing bouncing up and down like a lizard shaking its head.

Gazelle decided to go to the market few miles away, on foot to buy shoes. It was a large market, serving many adjoining towns and villages. He took off early to get there before the market was in full session. It took him an hour to reach his destination, walking steadily at a steady pace and singing to himself as the road was lonely at that time of the morning.

Now in the market, he met people who he knew, they talked and made merry. He eventually found the shoes he wanted, bargaining hard and eventually purchased them. He caught up with his friends again and together they moved to a restaurant situated in the centre of the market square to enjoy a breakfast of roasted yam and palm oil, as there was nothing else to choose from on the simple menu.

They moved from there to a palm wine parlour where they spent several hours knocking back the palm wine and dancing to music performed by a popular local artist. He then decided to make his way home, using a different route; for he never used the same road to go back; it had to always be an alternative pathway.

He moved along at a good pace, carrying his shoes in one hand until he was halfway to his destination when he saw a vehicle bearing down on him from the opposite direction. He moved to the side of the road to give way, but the vehicle kept on driving towards him. He moved rapidly, like his namesake, into the bush and away from the road. The vehicle swerved into the bush and the driver and Gazelle were killed.

The well-to-do family of the person who had died while being chased by Gazelle had taken the law into their own hands and avenged the death of their loved-one. He had never realised that he was being followed from the moment he left the house that morning, and that he had been continuously monitored the whole day whilst in the marketplace.

Gazelle's mother was devastated and distraught on hearing of the sudden death of her only son. She had lost her husband when she was in her twenties, having married him when she was only fifteen, pregnant and in Secondary school; much to the chagrin of her parents.

Following the death of her husband, Gazelle was all she had had in life and she adored and treasured him. People saw her everywhere with him. He was never out of her sight and they were inseparable. She was such a caring mother.

Now that he was no more, her life was empty for she had nothing left in this world to occupy her mind. It was so tragic, and she mourned over such a prolonged period that her neighbours and the villagers wondered whether she would survive her loss and began to worry about her welfare. She cried and cried for several weeks until she lost her voice and started croaking like a frog at night.

Neighbours were hurting so much themselves but still stayed with her, providing as much support as was humanly possible. They brought her cooked meals that she refused to eat and supplied shopping that piled up in her small bungalow, but to no avail. The burden of the loss of an only son wouldn't leave her.

In the early hours of every morning, neighbours and villagers would be suddenly woken up with a shudder because of loud crying filtering down from the top of a hill where Gazelle's mother lived, and they would also start weeping as they were equally traumatised. This nightly ritual went on for so long that the suffering villagers now at their wits' end wondered how it would end.

Unfortunately, there was, for one Saturday night, in the early hours of the morning, there was no sound of crying from the hilltop bungalow. The villagers and neighbours now dumbfounded, rushed up the hill in large numbers to find Gazelle's mother assuredly dead, with tears in her eyes.

The villagers could not contain themselves. They threw themselves down on the ground beside her, crying and screaming wildly for hours on end, unable to console each other. It was a harrowing scene. They all had tensely distressed looks. It was no longer the village they knew so well; tragedy had hit them; it was like an unbearable blow to the head.

Chapter 16

Okafor, Nwadibia's uncle, was a village farmer who came to stay with Nwadibia for a time. The main reason for the visit was for a medical check-up as he had been diagnosed with prostate cancer two years previously. It now seemed that the cancer had spread but this needed to be confirmed. He was booked in for a bone scan at the Radiology Department situated at the end of the Government Hospital building away from the normal flow of traffic, to lessen radiation exposure to the public.

On the day of his appointment, he arrived at eight a.m., accompanied by Nwadibia. At the reception, they were briefed on details of the test. It involved an intravenous injection of radioactive material followed by a couple of hours waiting to allow the radioactive agent to be taken up by the bones.

Following the long wait, full-body images were obtained using a gamma camera that picked up the radiation to build a picture of the uptake of the radioactive material in his bones. Whilst Nwadibia was in the department, he took a keen interest in the various posters on the walls and bombarded staff with questions relating to the test. It was during this loitering about in the Department that he noticed an advertisement on the wall for a cleaner.

Some years ago, he was able to identify the boy, Timothy, who had been observing him when he was in a compromising position in his room upstairs where he lived with his girlfriend. He told Timothy that he would forgive him, but a time would come when he would need his services. This idea surfaced in his mind again, so clearly that he wondered if this was an opportunity to contact him, now that he was fully grown.

Timothy, slim, tall and endowed with a face that projected self belief, had undergone a rapid growth spurt and became gigantic at the early age of fourteen. He had an enigmatic personality. How he had acquired the perfect use of the English language remained a mystery for he had not attended school and was not taught privately by anyone. He was blessed with great intelligence and language skills.

His background was not detailed but it was understood that he had lived in a house with four flats. An excellent English language teacher, a single mother with three small kids lived in one of the flats. She struggled with her teaching job, as she had to care for her children single-handedly, at the same time.

Timothy, living in the same quarters, was a ten-year-old, who spent a lot of time with the children. The teacher, Emily, read children's books profusely and unfailingly to her offspring. Timothy was ever present, listening to Emily's beautiful reading in her sexy, smooth and resonating voice.

The children often fell asleep during the stories, but she kept on reading. He took everything in from the reading as he was gifted with enormous intellect and memory. When the children became older and able to read, Emily bought several books to match their ages and took time to teach them to read while Timothy watched and learnt with the kids.

When Emily was away during the day teaching at her school, he took over and read for the toddlers in a lovely public-school accent, as if he had just graduated from Oxford University. At the age of fourteen, Timothy had developed enviable communication and reading skills, through his own diligence and persistence.

Nwadibia approached Timothy, who was now in his twenties, and asked him to apply for the cleaning job in the Radiation Medicine Department. Timothy quietly listened to the request and left, saying nothing. He got home, thought carefully about it and hesitated for days before applying for it. At the verbal interview for the job, he mesmerised the members of the interview panel with his command of the English language and his disarming accent. He was given the job on the spot.

On his first day, he was well-briefed on the dangers of being exposed to ionising radiation and the three cardinal principles of radiation: the importance of keeping a safe distance from the radioactive sources, the need to spend as little time as possible with the radioisotopes for the less time spent, the less radiation was absorbed and finally the importance of shielding oneself to minimise the exposure.

He took everything in and was not fazed. He was over-interested, and no doubt excited about his cleaning job and he dug into it in a big way. He began to appear even when not needed in areas of activity, pretending to be mopping the floor with his brush on a long stick, wearing a lead protective yellow apron and gloves. He would suddenly appear in places where he was not even allowed to be, watching and taking in information irrelevant to his job, totally ignoring his well-detailed job description.

On a typical day, Radiation Medicine staff that were specially trained in handling radioactive material would go into a special room to prepare the radiopharmaceuticals needed for tests on that day. The room housed various isotopes of different radioactivity. The radiopharmaceutical technicians were painstakingly careful, requiring concentration and a lot of calculation to prepare the correct dose of the substance to avoid exposing patients to unnecessary radiation. Only two of the personnel had this training.

It was usually done early in the morning when the department was quiet, and they were able to work without distraction. Timothy, however, would suddenly appear with his trademark brush on a long stick, in the restricted area meant for these specialised individuals. The radioactive substances involved most often were for medicinal purposes, mainly used for radiological investigations and treatment. When required for medical imaging as in this case, It was drawn into a syringe which was enclosed in a lead shield and ready to be injected.

In the waiting room, patients began to trickle in to be injected with the substance and then were expected to wait for a couple of hours before whole body images were taken as described previously. Timothy would again show up in the injection room; his timing was impeccable.

The trained nurses, in their protective gowns, had a delicate job to perform. The spilling of a single drop of the radioactive substance on the floor would have led to an emergency clean-up operation and painstaking decontamination. Nevertheless, Timothy would bombard them with questions at this time.

Timothy was becoming a real nuisance in the workplace. To make his behaviour more annoying and intolerable, he would stand in the reporting room in the afternoon, pretending to be doing his job while Radiation Medicine Doctors did their reporting, analysing bone scans mounted on white X-ray film boxes as the Doctors pointed to the areas of abnormal radioisotope uptake in the bones to students training in Radiation Medicine.

He saw it all and even began to read textbooks relating to the specialty, left carelessly lying around by students in the briefing room. Timothy spent six months at his cleaning job, and then one day he disappeared from the department, and was seen no more. He just vanished without a trace. No one in the department was able to work out why Timothy was just literally lost from view. All sorts of speculation filled the air. His sudden absence from work remained a puzzle for months on end. They were blindsided on his disappearance.

Chapter 17

Nwadibia had hated his time in prison and his being ill-treated by society. As he understood it, the person who should really have been incarcerated was the London-trained lawyer, Eze, who had no regard for human life. After all, Nwadibia had only tried to bring into focus the way this callous, unconscionable individual was killing pedestrians on the road like animals. His appearance in court was most painful, for it exposed his own dastardly and clandestine activities. He wondered what was left now. He sought vengeance.

Eze, having recovered from his ordeal and humiliation, resumed work in the high court as a lawyer, winning case after case. He was now becoming more popular with the population who had previously despised him as they felt that he was a bit stuck up and did not mingle with his own people. They possibly forgave him as a result of the humiliation that had occurred publicly. He took a long vacation and travelled to the United Kingdom to meet up with a white girl, Emilia who also studied law. They had been in the same class together.

They had gotten on very well and eventually they became friends. Both were academically proficient and there was such fierce and unhealthy competition between the two for the top score that it nearly put paid to their relationship. Both gained first class degrees, after which their relationship began to blossom. They could be seen most evenings in the London streets, holding hands, going into restaurants for glorious meals, and hopping from pub to pub.

This London visit had served him well for it was an opportunity to meet up with Emilia. She was really excited; for it had been over four years since they had last seen each other. She had missed him immeasurably, but she bottled it up and kept it to herself. The day they finally met, when she saw him approaching from the side street, she ran so fast and jumped up in the air to steal a kiss, a kiss so fitting the occasion that it made her wet, which was very unusual for her.

They dashed into a nearby restaurant, seated themselves comfortably and began talking and catching up with events of the past years. Both had turned up beautifully dressed, but this was unintentional. They spent over three hours in the restaurant wining, dining and relaxing; moreover, they had a lot of catching up to do.

The place was gradually filling up with diners when suddenly Eze went down on his knees to ask Emilia if she would marry him. The old clock on the wall momentarily began to chime, all eyes now turned towards her as she began crying and before she could say a word in the dim lighting, Eze had slipped the gold ring on her finger in one quick, slick move. At this time the chiming clock fell silent.

Those around the restaurant, watching such a landmark event were moved and overjoyed, and responded by screaming, waving and shouting words of approval. He soon rose up and both hugged each other for a long time before bringing it to an end with a warm kiss coinciding with enthusiastic clapping of hands from the dining crowd.

Emilia was a sweet girl; private school educated and from a middle-class family. Her parents were wealthy practising lawyers who lived in a large house located on several acres of well-kept land. They were disliked by neighbours who considered them to be proud and haughty.

Emilia had had a tough time in school because of her posh English accent and her aristocratic parents. She was constantly bullied and consequently she kept on changing schools. She found it difficult to make friends and was often considered to be different from her peers because of her privileged background. Lacking friends made her bury herself in books, constantly seeking new knowledge.

Emilia worked hard, delving deeply into her assignments and became a star student. A few in her class tried to emulate her but to no avail; they were incapable of catching up with her and as a result, they were filled with jealousy and hatred for her.

One time, she went out to a bar drinking with her mates the night before an important examination. The night progressed and they ended up at a nightclub. They were there for quite a while chatting, drinking and making merry, when her favourite music came on. She suddenly dropped the drink she held in her hand onto the table and danced her way into the dance floor.

She was a joy to watch for she was such a good dancer with her effortlessly smooth movement of her well-shaped waistline and wonderfully straight, smooth long legs that mesmerised both sexes.

When her favourite music ended, she went back to her seat and finished her drink, not realising that it had been tampered with by her mischievous so-called friends. Within an hour, she collapsed into unconsciousness and was rushed to hospital.

Emilia missed her examination and had to repeat the whole year. Her parents did not take kindly to the wicked behaviour of her mates and decided to take the principal of the school to task. Emilia was moved to another school, several miles away.

The pair had a wild time in London, as the summer-time weather was pleasantly warm and bright. Most of the time was spent outdoors shopping and gathering stuff for the upcoming wedding. They looked like a couple in a rush. In their excitement to shop together, they splurged about a thousand pounds, buying things they might not have needed, for in retrospect, they had forgotten to make a list beforehand. Even her wedding dress was not given careful thought. They walked into a shop that sold such dresses; saw about four people admiring one easily likeable dress and the two snagged it. When they got home, they discovered to their disappointment that it did not fit. They had to return it in the end and exchange it for a better fitting but more expensive one. Eze had to spend an extra six weeks in London so they could travel back together. She needed a month to resign and leave her job at a big law firm.

She had made her mark in her department and progressed rapidly, arriving early at work for she was a punctilious individual and she was the last to lock up and leave the office. Her departure had an immensely negative impact on the law firm and was taken badly by her superiors and co-workers, but they eventually conceded that one had to move on in life.

Chapter 18

Emilia eventually arrived to live in the Nigerian town of her partner. Obviously, the city was new to her and she was welcomed well by a multitude of people and had to swiftly adjust to the local customs. She also had to cope with a lot of other things, for example, it took her time to get used to the peppery cooked meals often prepared for her.

Her mother-in-law did not welcome her for she had expected her only son to marry an indigene; not a white girl. In short, she disliked her a great deal and she went out of her way to make her stay very short. She would purposely put too much hot spices in her food, particularly in soup and stew.

At mealtimes, as Emilia ate, she would constantly be suffering from eating all that pepper, but she could not find a way to extricate herself from the constant hurt she experienced while having the cooked food. Her mother-in-law would watch from a distance with glee, hoping and falsely believing that the unpleasantness Emilia was experiencing would send her packing back to England.

One other problem for Emilia reared its head in church during her first Sunday mass. As Emilia walked into the church with her partner the other parishioners, especially the women, were eyeing her angrily instead of warmly welcoming her. The cold reception was obvious to both of them, but they could not fathom what the problem was. Nevertheless, they quietly sat down and endured the discomfort. The parishioners took their time and waited for the right time to achieve the maximum effect.

The Sunday service progressed smoothly, until it was time for communion and all eyes were on Emilia. Their timing was perfect. As Emilia tried to get up to go for communion, she was so shouted down for not wearing a head band to cover her hair that she literally fell back into her seat like a small meteorite dropping suddenly from the sky.

The couple began to prepare for their wedding in earnest, by drawing up a guest list and a program for the wedding reception. They chose a popular hall in town as the reception venue. They had already been to see the Roman Catholic priest about three times, who went through the intricate process of what was expected from them as marriage partners. The priest also prepared them for the forthcoming church ceremony.

It was difficult to take everything in, but they pretended to have understood it all in order not to be thought of, as being dull or poorly schooled. They wouldn't have bothered so much if they had realised there would be a rehearsal of the church ceremony the evening before the actual wedding.

At this rehearsal, the priest took the bride and bridegroom to be and those who would be directly involved with the church ceremony through the whole process. Those who were to read the bible passages also took part, along with the best man. The best man was a childhood friend of Eze's and a confidant.

The morning of the wedding was like any other day, heralded by a beautiful sunlit sky and the singing of early morning nesting birds. A beautician arrived early to tend to the hair of the bride and bridesmaids. It took ages and by the time it was done, it was almost time to leave for the church, for punctuality was of the essence.

The priest did not tolerate latecomers. The church was already filled when the bride arrived. It was the same church that Nwadibia and his henchmen had visited often, and where they had tormented and tortured the parishioners for years, stealing from them. It was a historic building, standing on smooth ground with no boundaries, stretching for quite a distance.

The church interior was well-decorated in meticulous detail with admirable and very artistic work. When inside this magnificent structure, you would be taken aback, feeling that you were already in heaven, but you were actually far from it. When you eventually gathered your senses, you would realise that you were still on this bloody earth where there was no escape from hardship.

With the church now fully packed, the atmosphere of celebration was palpable. Women took centre stage in various attire competing with each other, in different coloured dresses, topped with mouth-watering headgear in different shapes and sizes. A whirlwind of events nearly derailed the wedding.

The touts in the motor park happened to get wind of the wedding and passed the information to Nwadibia who immediately swung into action. Things would soon get messy for revenge was sweet when served cold, he mused.

The religious wedding ceremony took off in good time with so much expectation in the air. The place was hushed when the priest showed up. The bride and groom by then, were seated on the front church pews but something was amiss, and the silence was disquieting and uncomfortable. This intensified as the bridegroom continually looked back in the direction of the aisle with much anxiety.

Everyone waited, including the priest; a sucker for punctuality. It had now been over thirty minutes of anxious waiting for his friend, on this most important day of his life, not knowing that his closest friend and best man was no more; liquidated in the early hours of the morning.

Fingers pointed without doubt to the notoriously violent Nwadibia. The best man was dropping his newly engaged, vivacious girlfriend back home on the night before the wedding but as they got to the front of her house, they were confronted by touts and, following a brief altercation, he was stabbed in the chest. He died instantly and the group just melted away.

He was a newly qualified Medical Doctor, whose eight siblings had hoped that he would support them in order to survive. Their elderly parents were so very poor and literally lived from hand to mouth for five years for him to train at the medical school. His death was a devastating blow to the frail parents, who had now lost the will to live. It was too much for the parents to bear. They also instantly lost the ability to cry.

The bridegroom, with the waiting guests becoming unnerved, suddenly walked down the aisle, humiliated, looking from side to side. It was such a pitiful situation for the bride who soon started weeping openly. The bridegroom, now getting to the middle of the aisle, saw a handsome young man in a well-tailored suit. He bent down close to this stranger and implored him to stand in for the absent best man.

The tall, elegant and well-educated priest opened the church service with a short, masterful speech. Things now began to move smoothly but when it got to the first reading, the first reader, who had participated in the rehearsal the previous evening, was nowhere to be seen and a substitute was scrambled for at the last minute.

They found themselves in a similar situation with the second reader. The two people absent had been picked up in different locations on their way to church. Unknown to all, during the rehearsal, Nwadibia had planted two people inside the church, making it possible for the sudden death and disappearances of the individuals in question.

More headaches were to rear their head soon after the church service. All the guests, five hundred strong, slowly drove down to the reception, five miles away. The venue was a large building with a spacious hall capable of accommodating all who had been invited but it was not to be; for while they were busy in the church four hundred and fifty undesirables in borrowed designer suits had taken over the seats to cause maximum unpleasantness to the bride and groom for the couple's guests now had to stand.

It had now, without doubt, become the worst day in the newlyweds' lives. It was such a painful situation for the bride who again started to cry her eyes out, because of the indescribable position she found herself in.

The proceedings inside the hall became so rowdy as a result of overcrowding and the speeches were drowned out by the deliberately noisy sounds. What a wedding that was, all her multitudinous guests were left standing – imagine! What a wedding! The disruption was unbearable and left a bitter aftertaste in the mouth.

Chapter 19

Tego was given a new identity and re-housed following his testimony against Jabbar. He was heavily guarded at an undisclosed address. He worked undercover and was assigned to a new duty that made him work in the office rather than out on the streets, to reduce exposure and the chance of unwanted recognition. The arrangement seemed to be working and he existed incognito for a while, but this stable situation was soon overtaken by circumstances beyond his control.

His father died suddenly in his hometown and the news broke his heart as he was very close to him. He took his death so badly that he was left devastated. Attending his burial outside his base was problematic because it was traditionally an open event, so that people from all over could attend to pay their respects.

He was so well protected and disguised that it was impossible to recognise him; moreover, the burial took place at night in darkness as there were no streetlights. After the funeral, he was driven by police escort to a hotel noted for its tight security and booked in under a false name.

Once he walked into his room in the quiet hotel, the police presence ended. He was resting in this large well-furnished room when around midnight he felt thirsty and wanted a drink. It being so late at night, he assumed that the bar would be free of people. He was wrong, for as soon as he got to the bottom of the steps that faced the lounge next to the bar, a man shouted his name in excitement, because the person was surprised to see him.

Tego did not recognise him but it seemed that the gentleman knew him, judging from his reaction and body language. Tego's spirit sank, as one would expect. He speedily paid for a bottle of water and beat it back to his hotel room. He sat down on the edge of his bed looking forlorn and out of sorts, screaming, "Oh my God, oh my God, my cover is blown! I'm a dead man walking!"

The next day, the police vehicle taking him back to base was followed and his new home was located. from that point on, he was trailed without his knowledge. Events moved quickly for he was now obviously a person of interest to someone, unbeknown to him. A chance meeting with a girl called Lovina would change everything, with far reaching consequences.

Lovina was a complex character; well-educated but she disguised it in every way, at a chance meeting, you would assume to your cost that she had never even received a basic education. She had in fact attended the best university in the country, obtaining a first-class degree in political science, yet she never mentioned it in conversation.

She was clever, sweet and tender but all of that was a disguise. It was not her true character. She was as deadly as a scorpion. Men were easily drawn in by her beauty, for she had a perfect figure: tall, elegant and adorned with the most attractive slanting green eyes. She had had a brief relationship with Jabbar, but that had fizzled out.

She was vivacious and frequented nightclubs. She loved dancing and whenever she took to the floor; all eyes were on her for she was a great dancer and seemed to float gracefully as she danced, bringing out her wonderful shape and accentuating her attractiveness. She had recently been in touch with Jabbar's mates.

Tego, in trying to shake off his sadness following his recent bereavement decided to visit an out-of-town nightclub, still not realising that his every move was closely observed. In the nightclub, he sat quietly in a secluded area, watching people dance and listening to the music.

He had been in that position for hours when Lovina walked towards him dancing barefoot with a glass of whisky held precariously in her left hand. She greeted him nicely and said, "What is a nice man like you doing in a place like this? This place is very bad. Please hold my drink for me while I dance." He did just that and she returned to the dance floor. She was correct in her assessment of the club for it was riddled with call girls and frequented by soldiers.

She continued going back to Tego to chat briefly to him and at the same time sip the drink he was holding for her. Past midnight, people began to stagger out of the night club. Lovina, who specialised in one-night stands, willingly accompanied Tego to his car and they drove home.

Now in his well-furnished house, Lovina began her usual prolonged love making, starting with dancing with her partner that lasted for over an hour. This was followed by hard drinking. She only drank alcohol. Luckily, Tego had a wide collection of locally brewed whisky and palm wine. They carried on for another hour drinking to the extent that Tego was beginning to lose control of himself.

He sank heavily onto a cushion and immediately fell asleep. At that juncture, Lovina, always very cool and deadly, as cool as a cucumber before she opened the door for Timothy. He was carrying something sinister in a syringe housed in a lead casing and he sprayed the hazardous substance all over Tego from a few yards away. Both Timothy and Lovina smiling now disappeared into the night, the job on hand accomplished. Tego never recovered from the radiation exposure and lasted for only two weeks.

Chapter 20

Following the wedding fiasco, Emilia and Eze, her lawyer husband, began to settle down. She loved the large, white house that her husband had built. The ground contained an extensive front garden with well- kept flowers that were strategically planted to bring into focus the exquisite beauty of the terrace.

By the side of the building was a space that could take ten cars, though only one car was visible, looking lonely and weather-beaten. A black Alsatian paced aggressively around the huge compound like a male lion patrolling its territory. A large iron gate located at an angle by the side and facing a major road served as the entrance to the premises.

A small side building next to the gate provided accommodation for the security guards. There were rooms galore; each fitted with a bathroom and toilet. A purpose-built kitchen was often used as an office. Here, they were fond of doing their legal work, whilst looking after the meal that was being cooked. The dining area was situated close to the kitchen for easy access.

The master bedroom was extensive and well-constructed, with a wooden bed placed in the centre of the room. The huge, immaculately clean windows extended from the roof to the ground. A defective window, open on top was a few feet away from the head of the bed.

The bathroom was also large and well furnished, fitted with a sizeable L shaped bathtub placed in the middle. Four loudspeakers hung on the wall, allowing for music played in the sitting room to filter in uninterrupted. The wall of the bathroom was painted immaculate white to match the colour of the bathtub.

Initially, they slept together as a young couple but after some time Emilia could no longer tolerate his constant, loud snoring and had to move to an adjoining bedroom. She found it hard and lonely at first, sleeping on her separate double bed. She wished that her husband was by her side, caressing, hugging and kissing her. At times, particularly in the middle of the night, she wished he was with her, for good measure. The heavy, tropical rain pounding the roof like mad, would have allowed her to scream loudly yet unheard at the height of her excitement.

Emilia gradually resumed her legal practice, appearing in court with her husband. She initially found it difficult and unsettling. She was uncomfortable with the crowded court room for she found it intimidating and at the same time suffocating. It made her nervous and insecure, even though her husband was by her side.

She lost her first case simply because she was not well-grounded in her new country's legal system and her voice could not be heard, compounded by her foreign English accent. She was speaking as if she had water in her mouth. People in court were stretching their necks continuously and were forced to cock their ears in order to hear her. To put it simply, she was completely inaudible and incoherent. She felt it herself and her pride was wounded.

When they finally got home, her husband noticed she was a bit withdrawn and taciturn. He tried all sorts to lift her mood but to no avail. He then decided to take her out for a meal as a last resort at a famous restaurant downtown, to be spoiled with her favourite meal of fish and chips topped with salad.

They hurriedly dressed up. Emilia put on her most-loved gown which brought out her wonderful curves and made her look like a star or a catwalk model. She looked so sweet in her pink platform shoes; they brought into centre of interest her delicately shaped legs which added to her striking beauty.

She was conscious of her good looks and obviously aware of side glances from her ever-present husband. On the other hand, her husband was wearing a conservative light dinner jacket over a multi-coloured silk shirt and designer trousers with a matching black belt. His shoes were brown, pointed and with a slightly raised heel which suited the occasion and made him look elegantly dressed. He looked extraordinarily fashionable, in a way that was pleasing to him.

The restaurant was packed when they arrived but there was no problem finding a table. They were wise enough to book in advance just before they left the house. They both sat down and ordered a bottle of red wine while they waited for the main meal to be served. As they drank and chatted, it became apparent that Emilia had not switched off yet and still wanted to bring up events that had taken place in court that had humiliated her.

Her husband was up to the mark by unexpectedly kissing her in such a romantic way that she forgot everything that was upsetting her. Their meal arrived and they both tucked into it and made sure that their plates were empty. By this time the bottle of wine was also empty. For the road, they ordered two cups of coffee topped with a tot of brandy for good measure.

As they relaxed, they began to talk about a few quirky law students in their class, particularly the one who continually stole books in the library as they watched him but was eventually caught red handed as he tried to jump from the window to escape. They laughed so much at this point for they had found it so hilarious when Emilia described how his large bottom was sticking out as his trunk was perched precariously on the window.

This pilfering individual, Etim, had a young wife but unfortunately both were cut of the same cloth. Emilia told her husband the bit he did not know and never would have imagined. She said she went to the best pub in London for a meal one weekend with this strange couple and they were seated. Next, she saw Etim pass two expensive designer wine glasses and cutlery from the table to his partner who put them into her handbag on her lap under the table.

Embarrassed, Emilia expressed her surprise to the couple, but the rest of her mates who sat at the same table told her that she 'ain't seen nuthin yet'. Etim and his wife then settled down laughing and told Emilia how they had stolen a whole television set from a shop in a busy shopping centre.

Chapter 21

When the couple got home, they continued to make merry, opening a bottle of whisky. They sat in the lounge, with classical music playing in the background when the man of letters decided he wanted to play scrabble with Emilia. The game was going smoothly when a long, high-scoring word arose. The problem was that it had been in use generally for a few years but could not be found in the Oxford dictionary.

The lawyer, trailing behind on points, refused to accept the strange word and a heated argument ensued, which quickly escalated. Emilia became so enraged that she threw the scrabble board on the floor with a deft movement and stormed off, fuming, into her bedroom.

Eze sat there motionless, wondering how such a relaxing evening could be ruined by a simple game. He sat there listening to Beethoven's Symphony, while struggling to finish his remaining glass of whisky. He staggered upstairs into his bedroom, changed into his night gown, and quickly went to bed and in no time was heard making a grunting sound loudly while asleep, by Emilia.

Emilia, on the other hand, was lying across her bed with her head buried in her pillow, sobbing quietly in her full regalia, burdened and saddened by her poor performance in court. Now the falling out with her husband seemed to have made her situation untenable. She was aggravated and inflamed at the same time.

Nwadibia was busy plotting and determined to deliver his revenge 'on a platter of gold'. The day had been spent with his friends in a remote bar hidden from view. The atmosphere was rowdy as the topic shifted from one subject to the other until it settled on the last football match, which his employed football hooligans had put paid to.

They debated vehemently under the influence of alcohol, about what the outcome would have been had the game been completed. The majority felt that the game would have been won by the local team. A few who belonged to the other side of the fence were verbally abused, punched and had palm wine thrown at them, before they were physically bundled out of the bar, bleeding and bruised. The rest continued to discuss other subjects. They switched to folktales; some of the stories were sad, interspersed with moments of sweet humour.

Nwadibia was a mysterious and remarkable criminal. He was little understood and thus was able to evade capture. He was an oddball. He had no schooling whatsoever; an illiterate, unable to read or write but understood the principles of radiation, even as a teenager. How that could be possible, he alone knew the answer. What he did twenty years ago would amaze and shock anyone. He was wickedly intelligent but, unfortunately his sharp intellect was directed towards evil.

His father had a long-running dispute with a successful farmer living in the same village, and he was determined to finish the farmer off. He wanted it done in a clean way, leaving no suspicion or trace to avoid the wrath of the villagers. Who else would he turn to but his deadly son, Nwadibia who instantly came up with the idea of using a rare poisonous plant he wrongly assumed had radioactive properties for he thought it was grown on radioactive soil. As a result, it was not easily available.

He had to go to a distant place where he plucked the leaves growing on a rocky hill. He quickly attached the leaves still on a branch onto a long stick, holding it up in the air to reduce possible radiation exposure to himself. He even knew the more distance one kept from a radioactive source, the less the radiation exposure would be.

Nwadibia, as huge as he was, perched on the victim's window like a bird, as he slept on his bed in the dead of night. He then held the deadly leaves placed at the end of the long stick over his father's enemy and waited for hours on end. Every night he appeared on the same spot for two weeks, but when nothing happened, he gave up disappointed at his wasted efforts. He used rat poison in the end, out of sheer frustration.

He left the bar in the early hours of the morning, having been well-entertained and fed with countless, witty stories he'd never heard previously. Eventually, he stumbled into Timothy's apartment. When he emerged, he was seen carrying a long cane with an attachment at the end and headed towards Emilia's house where her husband was fast asleep, snoring away.

Nwadibia gained entrance through the back door, stretched up to drop his long cane onto the back balcony and scaled into the exact position his deadly possession was resting; luckily, it was undamaged. He popped the cane through the gap in the faulty window and extended it towards his victim, still snoring, oblivious to the danger he was in.

With a mischievous smile on his face, Nwadibia waited patiently for a few hours and left with his device held high away from himself. This routine was again repeated for upwards of seven days; secret nightly visits, like a night owl. It took only a week after his exposure to radiation for Eze, the famous lawyer to start to lose weight and by the end of the second week, he was like a skeleton. He was then rushed to hospital with an alleged cancerous tumour for no one knew exactly what had happened to him; people only derived comfort from pure speculation.

He was ghost-like and only lasted a few days in hospital. When the news of the death of the well-loved lawyer spread, Nwadibia heard of it and immediately went to celebrate in the remote wine bar he had visited recently. He got thoroughly inebriated, drinking too much locally made palm wine.

Chapter 22

Timothy was off on a final mission that would take him through several small towns to intended destination, fifteen miles away. He was not in a hurry, for the plan was to reach the location late at night. His bag was weighing him down. It was early morning, and as one would expect at that time of the day, the footpath was dead quiet and deserted.

He felt lonely and his mind began to wander. He suddenly remembered an incident that occurred in his teenage years that had traumatised him and left a permanent scar. One morning, his mother left for the market, leaving him and the maid behind. Normally, she would spend a whole day in this far-away market.

For some inexplicable reason, she suddenly returned to find Timothy on her bed on top of the house help. He could not escape quickly enough as he was taken unawares, and his mum began to flog him all over his naked body without pity. The punishment persisted for a lengthy period, and he began screaming, "Oh my God! Oh my God! Forgive me! She enticed me with fried plantains, Mama! Mama! You will kill me; you will kill me!"

Despite his pleading, the cane continued raining down on him until he passed out. He still bore the scars and each time he saw them; he would lose his cool and start weeping. He had deep feelings about the incident. He started crying now, forgetting he needed to concentrate as he was on a dangerous mission.

In his altered mood, he made a quick detour to look for something to lighten his mood and lift his spirits. It was fast approaching summer, a great time for festivities. He now remembered an initiation into girlhood ceremony taking place in an under-developed village away from his mapped-out route.

Within an hour, he reached it to find the festival in full swing; a mass of people in high spirits, a sea of smiling faces. It looked like the whole town had congregated in this large open square, everyone milling around, apparently aimlessly but with a sense of excitement.

Dance groups were all around, playing their drums frenetically and with great rhythm. Nude girls with beads around their shapely waistlines danced gracefully in tandem, with their bare, pointed breasts swinging in the wind.

The place was unique and atmospheric, teeming with people of all shapes and sizes. The men looking for wives faced these barely clothed teenage girls, eyeing them romantically. The suitors appeared amazingly healthy, muscular, youthful and full of life.

Timothy, thinking he was as handsome as the teenage boys, found himself a position in the line-up. He was quite the opposite, ugly in the real sense of the word, with a protruding nose on a tiny face; he had a false and exaggerated image of himself.

Nevertheless, he managed to capture a front position among these strong boys. His heavy, sinister bag weighed on his shoulder, almost enough to dislocate it. His behaviour was extremely bizarre. He remained in the square to the end, approaching night-time, as those gathered began to gradually leave for home.

He continued his onward journey and by the time he got to his destination, it was past midnight. The place of interest was a detached house occupied by a local chief. He was sent by Nwadibia to settle a twenty-year-old feud between the chief and Nwadibia's father. The occupant was a mischievous and compelling character, now in his seventies.

The details of the dispute were clouded in a bit of mystery but had to do with wife swapping that went drastically wrong when this villainous man walked off with Urdu's wife, who also happened to be Nwadibia's mother. Nothing now would satisfy Nwadibia except a cool execution. Who else could handle this job efficiently except Timothy, who prepared to accomplish his task, now fully determined, knowing that he was much closer to his target.

Having scaled the low fence in total darkness, he made for the dormant bungalow standing in the periphery of the compound, moving stealthily but quickly with a great deal of attention as he approached his main objective.

He prized open a low-lying weather-beaten wooden window and climbed into the chief's bedroom. He was fast asleep as one would expect at that time of the night. Timothy carefully opened his bag and dropped some of his lethal weapon, now out of its lead shielding and escaped into the night. He looked back with a smile on his face at the lonely figure in bed, soon to be a dead man; mission easily accomplished.

Chapter 23

Now with the bag lighter, although not empty at that point, he walked more comfortably and leisurely for several miles, along narrow roads and dangerous footpaths. He kept on for hours on end until day broke and darkness faded. He could now see exactly where he was going, hardly meeting anyone along the isolated routes.

It was in his mind to pass through the village of the initiation ceremony he had witnessed and participated in the day before. The previous day, he'd followed the girl he fancied as she walked into her compound, but she was not aware of him trailing (along) behind her. He had noted the location of her home in his head and then carried on to his destination.

Now on his way back, Timothy made for the girl's house. Had he not gone through this town, he would have been home and dry. His weakness for the opposite sex took control of him and his faculties.

He was now standing in front of her house, knocking on the door, a total stranger early in the morning in a rural area. The girl whom he had admired came to open the door with surprise on her face. She dashed back into her bedroom, calling her parents in a loud panicky voice, as she entered her bedroom.

Still standing in the middle of the passage, he was ushered into the sitting room when her father eventually came out, looking sleepy with both eyes half-closed. There was undisguised puzzlement on his face in trying to make sense of what this unusual visit meant.

Nevertheless, he made every effort to appear welcoming. They talked about various things including the recent festivities; their conversations were punctuated with humour and wit. The girl's mother, looking elegant in a pink flowing nightgown, now came out to greet Timothy and hurriedly went into the kitchen to make coffee for them.

With the parents now sitting together with Timothy having hot coffee, he declared his true intentions to them, floating the idea of marriage and a long-lasting relationship with their smashingly attractive daughter. They listened with calmness and great appreciation for their lovely child whom they were besotted with.

Timothy spent hours in the house and was treated to a sumptuous breakfast, which he consumed with speed as he had not eaten in the past twenty-four hours. With breakfast over, the teenage girl came to clear the dining table. At this point, both parents left the dining area on purpose to allow Timothy to address their daughter.

He opened the conversation, as she cleared the table. She listened intently but already knew what her answer was going to be, she had already made up her mind. She had one of the boys that lined up in the festival square the previous day in mind. She turned Timothy down immediately without preamble. Now feeling downcast and outrageously rejected, he hurriedly left the room, saying nothing to her or her parents.

As he left the house on his onward journey home, heavy clouds descended on the area. Lightning flashed and thunder broke the morning silence. In no time, it began to rain. It was a downpour that Timothy had never experienced before. The raindrops pelting him were as thick as tap water. It began to hurt his head and face so badly that he put his bag on his head to serve as an umbrella. He didn't consider the deadly contents of the bag on his head.

The path was so flooded that he was almost swimming as he struggled along. Visibility was so poor that he stumbled into shrubs alongside the path, and at times clashed with small trees. The final three miles was such hard going that he thought of giving up. When he finally arrived, he was near to death.

The unexpected adverse weather conditions soaked his deadly bag so much that the lead metal casing was flooded, causing a leakage of the material inside it. Timothy was inadvertently and continuously soaked with high activity radioactive material disguised as rain drops.

He got home, immediately went to the back garden and dropped his lethal bag in a twenty-foot deep hole dug in advance and filled it up with earth. By the time he staggered to his bedroom, he was very tired and worn out. He did not realise it was not just sheer exhaustion. He had now become seriously ill and was totally out of sorts.

Timothy was rushed to hospital but within three days he was no more. He did tell his immediate family, who had gathered by his bedside, about his secret mission and the person who had sent him on the errand.

Nwadibia was secretly told by his informants that Timothy had spilled the beans; he now knew he was in a lot of trouble and decided that his situation was dire and needed immediate action. He convened a meeting with haste. He met with his now depleted band of killers in the dead of night, in a small, dilapidated thatched hut with a sagging roof, almost touching the ground. Entry was made possible through a one-panel door, but the building was without windows. The owner had given no thought to ventilation.

They sat there in the dark, looking gloomy and downcast. This time the mood was tense, no one thought of having drinks. They spoke in low, pensive voices, almost bordering on whispering, as if they had completely lost the will to exist.

They deliberated for hours on end until a cock crowing at about four o'clock in the morning brought the crucial meeting to a close. In a nutshell, it was decided that remaining in the town was unsafe. They hurriedly left the city, travelling to various known locations. Nwadibia ended up back in his village he'd run from several years before, to evade capture.

Chapter 24

The new police chief, Marcus, had not yet made his mark. He had been in the post for nearly twelve months. He was beset with family problems and other issues of his own making. His wife of ten years was well-schooled but adamantly refused to seek employment. Rather, she opted to be a housewife, remaining at home, refusing to socialise with friends and neighbours alike.

She lived almost like a hermit but for her husband. She had a weakness for alcohol; a secret drinker, who only drank at home, stocking up on bottles of locally produced whisky, cleverly hidden out of sight in unusual spaces within the official police quarters where they lived.

Every time her husband got back from a hard day's work, he would find her in the lounge, lying on the floor practically comatose, with empty bottle of whisky by her side. The house remained forever unkempt and smelly. She was finding it difficult to keep up with housework and ignored her personal hygiene.

She was asked once by a medical doctor how much she drank. Her daughter was in attendance in the consulting room but kept quiet. The mother used two fingers to indicate clearly that she only had a tot of whisky in her coffee at bedtime.

Her daughter grimaced but said nothing for she seemed terrified and intimidated by her mother. She was cowering, judging from her body language. When both left the consulting room, her daughter hastily returned to the consultant, and out of earshot of her mother, whispered to the Doctor that her mother drank at least two bottles of whisky a day.

Marcus, now feeling unsettled due to his wife's behaviour, began to have a lot of girlfriends in various parts of town. He did away with his ten bodyguards to continue with his clandestine nightly visit to see his girlfriends.

Late one night, coming out of a night club, he made a quick decision not to go home but to visit his closest girlfriend. On getting to her flat, situated on the third floor of a multi-storey building, he found that the door was locked, and that she was with another man. He threw caution to the wind and started shouting at the girlfriend and the man with her. It was now a free for all, the three of them exchanging abusive words, two against one.

This took place in the early hours of the morning and lasted a long time. The altercation even spilled on to the street because when the police officer, Marcus got out of the building he kept on with the slinging match, shouting at the top of his voice, to match the loud voices coming from the third floor of the building. You could hear them from a mile away, in the dead of night.

Naturally, people were woken from their sleep to listen to the loud commotion. A crowd gathered on the street, frightened but amused. He called her names: whore, slag, husband-snatcher, shoplifter, ignoramus, one-night stand expert, etc. A few couples chuckled and at the same time sighed at being woken up from their sleep.

Unfortunately for Marcus, one person identified him, and the news of his misdemeanour appeared in the local newspaper the next morning, with his picture in the front page looking scruffy and weather-beaten. The incident damaged his reputation immeasurably. He never recovered from it. It was an event of his own making and there could be no excuse for it.

Marcus no doubt miscalculated and took the wrong decision when Tego was released from prison. He focused on the immediate capture and trial of Jabbar. He felt more comfortable dealing with one case at a time rather than crowding himself with a lot of information on different cases.

During debriefing, Tego only provided detailed information of what he knew about Jabbar, leaving out the other incriminating evidence relating to the other murderous prisoners he had shared the cell with. All was lost when Tego was suddenly bumped off. The bumbling police chief would live to regret such a shamble and his lack of judgement.

Nwadibia had ventured out of his accommodation only once since he had returned, fully disguised in a large bowler hat, and unrecognisable with his newly adopted peculiar gait, wearing one arm in a sling. He was stooped and shuffled in small steps at a slow pace. Information that he had moved to the village reached the chief inspector of police, Marcus, a month later.

He had to go back to the drawing board to work out how to proceed to bring the rest of this marauding gang to justice. When Nwadibia returned four hours later from his first outing, he was seen entering the football-field-sized compound through the only entrance available. He was spotted by an undercover police officer in plain clothes, hiding in a small bush with good visibility on the location of interest.

Nwadibia, being so cunningly clever, like most criminals with evil intent, veered off to the back of the building and then could not be seen, making it impossible to identify which building he had finally entered. There were over thirty similar buildings, identical in both size and shape, and almost impossible to differentiate. The wall of each building was made of clay, polished often to look clean and smooth.

Marcus now swung into action. Thirty elite combat police officers, experts in the use of firearms were assembled in a lecture hall one morning and addressed by the police chief. No one knew in advance the mission target. He stood by a blackboard and lectured them on every detail of the unusual compound and the strange characteristics of the wives living there. He showed them large drawings of the buildings therein.

One stupid, short police officer sat in the front row. He was looking so tired and worn out, having just got back from a nightclub, drunk. As one would expect, he fell asleep and to make his situation even worse, he was snoring so loudly that Marcus had no choice but to throw him out.

The snorer was so short that he should never have been in the police force but for the rampant corruption that was going on. Following this unwanted interruption. Marcus continued with his lecture, emphasising the importance of judgment and anticipation. His talk was interspersed with his own exaggerated achievements, told with sparks of humour.

He forgot that he had once tried to arrest a pickpocket in the town square years ago. The pick pocket threw a left hook which felled Marcus to the ground, knocking him flat on his face. He tried not to remember that; instead he remained ever so boastful. In his summary, he told the officers to shoot Nwadibia whenever he was sighted and that they should not take any prisoners.

At about five o'clock the next morning, on a cloudless Harmattan day, several police officers arrived at Nwadibia's huge property and surrounded the entire circumference of the compound.

They met a few scantily dressed teenage girls with bare breasts and empty clay pots on their heads. They were leaving this encircled compound, on their way to fetch water four miles away. They passed a few police officers who kept on looking at them. In fact, one enthusiastic constable boldly touched the breast of the most beautiful girl as she walked by. She bit his fingers so hard in one quick, smart movement. He yelped and bolted, whimpering like a dog.

The real job began in earnest. They started searching the huts one-by-one. They never realised it was a big mistake to start the search from the buildings closest to the entrance and then work their way downwards to the other end. They forgot they were dealing with a deadly criminal who lived far back and nowhere near the entrance of the compound. He had plenty of time to escape.

He had dug a tunnel with his bare hands the moment he arrived in the village. It took him several days to dig and get rid of the mud that piled up at a rapid pace. He worked day and night. It extended from his parlour to the back garden.. His informants stationed permanently at the entrance, came to let him know immediately they noticed police movements.

He crawled into the tunnel in a jiffy and disappeared into a thick jungle which stretched for about a mile, separating his village from the adjoining hamlet. Months later, he was still at large, along with his now depleted band of murderers. They were quite aware they remained hunted men. All the neighbouring towns and villages would continue to bleed from the nefarious activities of this criminal gang.

The town dwellers hoped that the police chief, Marcus, would get a head start and see that Nwadibia and his gang remained constantly on his radar. He was also expected to bring the populace up to speed on how the investigation was progressing. At some point they began to wonder if Marcus could keep the community in the loop regarding progress, as he now seemed less enamoured with the responsibility that was linked to his new post. His situation was made more difficult because his police officers were known by the general public to be on the take. It was now becoming a general feeling in the town that a new police chief was needed with Nwadibia still evading capture and free to strike again, at any time and place of his choice.

FÜR AUTOREN A HEART FOR AUTHORS À L'ÉCOUTE DES AUTEURS MIA KAPΔIA ΓIA ΣYΓ
FÖR FÖRFATTARE UN CORAZÓN POR LOS AUTORES YAZARLARIMIZA GÖNÜL VERELIM S
PER AUTORI ET HJERTE FOR FORFATTERE EEN HART VOOR SCHRIJVERS TEMOS OS AU
ÖINKÉRT SERCE DLA AUTORÓW EIN HERZ FÜR AUTOREN A HEART FOR AUTHORS À L'ÉCO
BCEЙ ДУШОЙ К АВТОРАМ ETT HJÄRTA FÖR FÖRFATTARE Á LA ESCUCHA DE LOS AUT
KAPΔIA ΓIA ΣYΓΓPAΦEIΣ UN CUORE PER AUTORI ET HJERTE FOR FORFATTERE EE
ÖINKÉRT SERCE DLA AUTORÓW EIN HERZ F
CÃO BCEЙ ДУШОЙ К АВТОРАМ ETT HJÄRTA F

The author

Dr John Anakwenze was born in Okwe, Nigeria. He
is a native of Abagana in Njikoka local government,
Anambra state. He qualified as a doctor in 1973
and practiced as a medical doctor from 1973–1976
before leaving Nigeria for United Kingdom for
postgraduate studies. He trained in Nuclear Medicine
in St. Bartholomew's Hospital in West London
between 1981–1983 and became well versed in
the use of radioactive substances for diagnostic
purposes and treatment. He returned to Nigeria in
1984, lecturing in Nuclear Medicine in the University
of Nigeria Teaching Hospital from 1985–1990. He
moved back to United Kingdom in 1990 with his
family. He is currently working in NHS hospitals as
a Locum Consultant in Geriatric Medicine. He has
written two nonfiction novels – A debut narrative
'The Bee Chase' and a sequel titled 'Udenka' quickly
followed.

The publisher

He who stops getting better stops being good.

This is the motto of novum publishing, and our focus is on finding new manuscripts, publishing them and offering long-term support to the authors.
Our publishing house was founded in 1997, and since then it has become THE expert for new authors and has won numerous awards.

Our editorial team will peruse each manuscript within a few weeks free of charge and without obligation.

You will find more information about novum publishing and our books on the internet:

www.novum-publishing.co.uk

John Anakwenze

The Bee Chase

ISBN 978-3-99064-243-6
110 pages

Death. Poverty. Rejection. Traitors. Udenka faces countless
hurdles as he grows up and tries to become a doctor in Nigeria.
Despite all he has been through, one specific memory from his
childhood is forever etched in his mind: the bee chase.

John Anakwenze

Udenka

ISBN 978-3-99064-444-7
126 pages

A great story about the struggles of a "doctor-in-training" in Nigeria during the Nigerian Civil War. John Anakwenze will fascinate anyone who is addicted to anecdotes about the trials of fighting your way up to becoming a doctor against overwhelming odds.